OUTER BANKS

OUTER BANKS

DEAD BREAK

JAY COLES

AMULET BOOKS

NEW YORK

Cataloging-in-Publication Data has been applied for and may be obtained from the Library of Congress.

ISBN 978-1-4197-6161-4

Text copyright 2023 Outer Banks TM/© Netflix
Book design by Deena Micah Fleming

Printed and bound in U.S.A.
10 9 8 7 6 5 4 3 2 1

Amulet Books are available at special discounts when purchased in quantity for premiums and promotions as well as fundraising or educational use. Special editions can also be created to specification. For details, contact specialsales@abramsbooks.com or the address below.

Amulet Books® is a registered trademark of Harry N. Abrams, Inc.

ABRAMS The Art of Books
195 Broadway, New York, NY 10007
abramsbooks.com

TO ALL *OUTER BANKS* FANS.
MAY THIS BOOK CAPTURE YOUR HEART
IN ALL THE WAYS IT DID MINE.

CHAPTER 1

KIE

"HELLO? ARE YOU THERE? I KNOW YOU SEE ME STANDING right in front of you!"

A big, burly man with a bald head is waving in my face. I'd seen him approach the counter I'm standing behind, but if I'm being honest, I kind of tuned him out until he snapped and cleared his throat at me loudly.

"Can I help you, sir?"

"I'd like a refill," he says, his voice a little raspy, shoving a clear cup in my face.

"Can you remove your straw, sir?" I try to keep the sass to a minimum; Dad says "the customer is always right" and all that, but it sneaks out from time to time.

He reaches forward and yanks it out. I'm not sure who pissed in this guy's cereal this morning.

"Diet Coke?"

"Coke Zero," he corrects.

I turn around, hiding my eyes as they roll to the back of my head. Diet Coke. Coke Zero. What's the difference?

The end of the school year and the beginning of summer break should have felt like some kind of victory lap. Particularly after the year I had, I deserve a summer filled with lazy mornings, friends, time in the water, and delicious, ice-cold treats that cool you down from all the heat. Summer break should be just that: a break. I'm desperately in need of one, especially after attending the Kook school, KCD (Kildare County Day School), all year long. My parents thought that KCD would straighten me out, put me on some "better path." All the Kookness made me want to vomit after the first week, let alone the full year. But summer break hasn't been much of a break from anything at all so far. Instead, summer's been more work than usual.

It's not like Mom and Dad gave me a choice. Waitressing at The Wreck for the summer for more hours than normal was part of the deal we made to get me back to public school in the fall. I thought it would be a small price to pay, all things considered.

But summer at The Wreck is the opposite of a break from Kookness. It might be even more Kook-filled than KCD, and that's saying a lot. Well, Kook- and tourist-filled. I'm not sure which is worse.

After filling up the drink, I hand it back to him and tell him to have a nice day. He grunts in return. Charming.

I wipe my hands on the apron tied around my waist, emblazoned with the restaurant's name. Other than the apron, we waitresses get to wear what we want, which for me means a black tank top and jean shorts. My dark hair is piled on top of my head, standard practice to prevent any stray curls from falling into people's food. At least I don't have to wear a hairnet like the folks who work in the kitchen (though Dad threatens to put me there from time to time if I can't be polite to customers). Hairnet or no, I'm not sure I'd mind. At least in the kitchen I could gossip with the chef and roll my eyes at the Kooks out front while accommodating their special requests: sauce on the side, dressing on the side, ice on the side. Sometimes I think they'd order their entire meals on the side if they could.

I glance at the clock above the entrance to the restaurant. One hour before my shift is up. If Pope was here, and if he was feeling as impatient as I am, he'd do the math: one hour, the equivalent of sixty minutes, or however many seconds, however many milliseconds, and on and on. (Unlike Pope, I can't do all that math in my head. Or I could, but I don't want to.)

My eye stops on the wall of posters and signs at the entrance to the restaurant, and I feel a thrum in my chest. My dream is to surf. If there's one thing I know I could do for the rest of my life, it's surfing. And not just for fun, but as a professional, with endorsements and a team and fans. A few weeks ago, some customer asked to put a flyer up on our local events wall at The Wreck. Annoyed, I waved him off and let him put his flyer up there. Later, walking by it, I saw that it was a call for surfers to enter a competition right here in our very own waters. I snatched the flyer off the wall and showed it to my parents that night at dinner, but between snide comments and being totally

3

ignored, it was clear they had no interest in letting me do it. But if there's anything I've learned about dreams, it's that they don't come true if you don't fight for them. And becoming a surfer is worth the fight.

After all, I've got nothing to lose.

The group sitting at one of our center tables gets up to leave, so I pull my gaze from the contest flyer, grab my tray and a rag to bus the table. The waitstaff has a long-running bet on who can bus tables the fastest. My best time so far is twelve seconds flat.

I clean the table in thirteen seconds this time. No record breaking today.

I turn around and let out a yelp that tightens up my whole body as I nearly collide with a tall guy who appears more like a brick wall.

"Oh, I'm so sorry," the guy says apologetically. He reaches for my shoulder but stops short of touching me, which is good. Dad doesn't like when I lecture the customers on boundaries.

I take a breath and get myself together, straighten myself out. "No problem, I'm fine. Just was caught off guard."

"Didn't mean to scare you," he says with a laugh, but I don't see what's funny.

"You didn't scare me." I've never seen this guy before. He has light brown eyes and dark brown hair that falls across his face like he doesn't have time for haircuts very often. He's wearing a bright tank top and jeans. He's definitely from out of town, and he's definitely not a Kook. Kooks don't apologize.

"Hey, do you, like, work here?" He has a slight foreign accent. It's subtle but there. And before I can answer or react at all, he catches himself. "Sorry, that's such a dumb question. You're wearing an apron and you just cleaned off a table. Of course you work here. Unless you're just the most generous person of all time."

"Yeah," I answer. "I work here." Usually, when I smile at the customers, it's all saccharine and aspartame, by which I mean it's artificial. But I can't help it; I'm flashing a real smile at this guy almost without realizing it.

"So . . ." he says.

I look up at him.

"Sorry, I just—can you tell me where the bathroom is?"

Oh, of course. That's why people talk to waitresses. I point him in the right direction, but I can't help watching him leave. He's got a lean, athletic build, his movements almost feline in their fluidity and grace.

That's when it hits me: This guy's a *surfer*.

The competition is just around the corner.

The contest is open to anyone: professionals, amateurs, wannabes, and everyone in between. Major surf competitions aren't usually held on the East Coast—our waves aren't nearly as big as those in other parts of the world—but apparently, the organizers of this competition wanted to prove that there can be serious surfing on this side of the globe.

Even though Dad has a strict no cell phones policy, I pull my phone from my pocket and sneak a peek at Surfline. The site is predicting a storm off the mainland that's going to bring bigger waves to the waters around the island, which means the competition won't just be paddle-in surfing but tow-in surfing as well. Which means surfers from around the world will be coming.

Here. To the OBX. Looking to catch monster waves.

I wonder if the guy who just bumped into me is one of them.

Dad shouts my name, and I stuff my phone back into my pocket. "Order up, Kiara! What are you doing on your phone?"

The thing I want to do most is lie, but Dad can fact-check me by looking at my phone history. "Just looking at stuff about the competition."

He grimaces. "Listen, Kiara, I know you really want to do this, but I don't think that's the best use of your time. We can talk more about it later, but for now, we've got hungry customers who have been waiting a while for their food."

I exhale loudly and walk away from him. I set a platter full of raw oysters on ice at table twelve and fried clam strips on table thirteen. I glance at the clock. *Tick, tick, tick.* Thirty minutes left to my shift.

Twenty-two minutes.

Eighteen minutes.

Did time always move this slowly?

Just when it feels like time has slowed to a standstill, I hear a whistle that can mean only one thing: John B, JJ, and Pope are approaching in the HMS *Pogue*. John B, JJ, and Pope are my closest friends—more like my mini-family—who often get me in a ton of unwanted trouble, but they're also who I have the most fun with and they always have my back. All four of us are close, but John B and JJ have known each other the longest, having grown up together more like brothers than friends.

They pull up to the dock outside the restaurant, and John B tosses me a rope. John B is wearing a short-sleeved button-down that's not actually buttoned, showing his chest and abs. That's the thing about John B: either he's shirtless or he's wearing something that shows his chest. I've never asked him about that, but if I were a guy and had abs, I'm sure I'd do the same.

"To what do I owe this pleasure?" I ask in a mock posh voice. Dad would love if I talked to customers that way. "Even Pope has decided to grace us with his presence."

Pope's spending his summer working, too, and he's working even more hours than I am. Not that he's actually getting paid. He has an internship at the local morgue, which would be weird for anyone except for Pope. For him, it makes perfect sense.

Sometimes I'm jealous of Pope. Both of his parents are Pogues. Both of his parents are Black. Both of his parents support his dream, or, at least, they seem to.

JJ's lounging across the back of the boat, but he pushes his sunglasses up to the top of his head and raises his eyebrows, bleached even blonder than usual by the summer sun.

"You see Surfline?" he asks.

"Yes!"

"Think you might try tow-in surfing?" JJ sits up straighter, his blond hair flowing in the wind. John B rolls his eyes as he secures the boat to the dock. JJ's got skills on the water, but he doesn't always remember to offer to help. John B wipes his forehead with the handkerchief wrapped around his wrist.

"I've only ever paddle-surfed, JJ," I answer. "I wouldn't have any chance of winning the tow-in competition."

"See?" JJ leans back in his seat. "This is why I don't think surfing should be competitive. It's all about the *experience*, not the medals."

"The prize isn't a medal, JJ. It's twenty thousand dollars."

JJ's eyes are already big, but they get even bigger. That's almost enough money to make him rethink his stance on whether surfing should be competitive.

John B says, "Maybe we should all enter. Four surfers have higher odds of winning than one. We could split the prize money evenly, whoever wins."

"You sound like Pope, calculating the odds," JJ says with a laugh, his smile revealing dimples.

"Five thousand apiece sounds good," Pope says. "But you forget, I don't really surf. Not like you guys." Of the four of us, Pope is the one who probably least enjoys being out on the water. But Pope's probably the smartest and the most talented out of all of us. He can do a little bit of everything. I like that about him.

"You sure you were born on this island, Pope?" JJ teases. "'Cause sometimes you sound like you grew up on the mainland."

I hear the sound of Dad clearing his throat behind me. That's his wordless way of saying that I'm not supposed to spend my shift hanging out with my friends.

"Hi, Mr. Carrera," Pope begins, but Dad isn't interested in the Pogues, not even when they're trying to be polite.

"Why don't you bring some of those boxes from the back to the bar, Kiara?"

"My shift is almost over!" I protest, but Dad's expression is stern.

"And you three"—Dad nods at the other Pogues—"this dock is for *paying* customers."

JJ stands and winks. "We'll be out of your hair in no time, Mr. C. Just wanted to use the bathroom."

"Also for paying customers," Dad begins, but JJ's already hopped out of the *Pogue* and followed me into the restaurant.

But instead of heading for the bathroom, JJ follows me into the storage room, where Dad's stacked cases of wine bottles and liquor for the summer menu.

"Is this what heaven looks like?"

"Very funny, JJ."

He grabs a bottle of my dad's premixed sangria before I can stop him and races for the door.

"JJ!" I shout.

Dad keeps close inventory over his supplies. He'll know JJ stole. I run after him, but JJ's already on the *Pogue*, and John B is already untying the rope from the dock.

9

Crap.

The alarm on my phone starts to buzz. My shift's finally over.

I don't hesitate. I run down the dock and leap onto the *Pogue* just as John B turns on the engine.

"Saved by the bell," I say.

"Just tell him the bartender's stealing from him."

"I'm not going to get some innocent employee in trouble just to help you cover up your crimes, JJ."

JJ rolls his eyes, then takes a swig of his contraband. He pulls a face.

"How bad can it be?" John B asks.

"Picture grape juice mixed with sour trash can juice," JJ says. He passes the bottle to John B.

"It's not bad," John B says, thoughtfully taking a sip.

"My dad's specialty. It's called the Island-tini," I explain. "Merlot mixed with club soda and slices of pineapples. He worked really hard on that name. Kooks love it."

"It sounds like something a Kook would drink. Fizzy and fancy, yet dry. I don't like the way it makes my throat feel like a carpet is rubbing against it over and over again."

"Kooks don't know what a good drink is, I tell you," JJ adds. "Kooks don't understand life."

"What do you mean?" I ask him.

"They don't know what fine dining is. A nice hot dog with mustard and a PBR. Not some nasty merlot and a loaf of meat they eat in some fancy restaurant at one of the hotels."

"Fish," I correct.

"What?"

"Kooks are here for fish, not meat."

JJ shrugs. "Whatever."

I plop down next to Pope in the back of the boat. "You think if I won the competition, my parents would let me quit The Wreck?"

Pope runs a hand over his close-cropped hair. "I doubt it."

"Maybe serving Kooks wouldn't suck so much if I knew I had twenty K in the bank." I lean back, releasing my hair from its work-ordered bun. Pope laughs as my curls brush against his chin.

"If I tell you something, will you promise not to tell them?" Pope nods in the direction of JJ and John B.

"Promise," I say, crossing my heart like I did when we were little.

He tilts his head down and leans close so I can hear him over the roar of the engine when he whispers, "I wouldn't quit my job for all the money in the world."

CHAPTER 2

POPE

"SO, HOW'S YOUR INTERNSHIP GOING, POPE?" KIE ASKS. WE'RE hanging out at the Chateau, which is kind of like our home away from home. It's got a huge backyard, a hot tub, and a lot of pictures of John B as a baby with his dad. We're sitting on the patio, just talking and hanging out. The bottle of Island-tini is long gone, but I can still taste it in the back of my throat, like sour cherries.

"I'm loving it. It's hard work, but I'm learning so much."

"Like what?" Kie sounds genuinely curious. She gets me in ways JJ and John B don't.

"Like, I always thought that your hair and nails kept growing after you die."

"They don't?"

"Nope," I answer. "What actually happens is the human body dries out, so that nail beds and skin on the head retract, making it look like your nails and hair are longer."

"That's interesting," Kie says, so I keep going.

"And you pee and poop a lot—like *a lot*—when you're dead for a while."

That's when JJ jumps in. "I don't want to think about pooping when I'm dead."

"You won't be thinking about *anything* when you're dead, silly, because you'll be dead," Kie says reasonably. She turns back to me. "What else have you learned, Pope?"

"Some dead bodies make really loud groaning noises."

JJ makes a *wooooo* sound like a ghost, but I shake my head.

"It's not creepy! It's science. It's because of all the gases trapped inside the body."

"How does that make it less creepy?" JJ responds incredulously. "That gives me the creepy-crawlies all over my skin!" JJ scratches his arms fiercely like a little kid who just got a taste of his first horror movie.

"Want to know one more fun fact about death?" I ask.

"No!" JJ and John B shout, but Kie shouts, "Yes!" even louder.

"There's a legit chance one of us could die by spontaneously combusting at any moment," I say. "It's terrifying, but also really, really cool, right?"

JJ and John B shake their heads like crazy, but Kie smiles at me. "It all sounds very . . . Pope-ish. I'm glad you're enjoying it." I love Kie's smile. It's one of the best ever.

"Moving on to something less freakin' gross . . . You guys ever name stars when you were a kid?" JJ asks all of us. I roll my eyes good-naturedly.

"I can't say I have," Kie says.

"Same," I add.

"I did once," John B answers. "But I didn't know you did, JJ. I've known you since the third grade, and I'm just now learning this?"

"I'm a man of many mysteries," JJ replies. "John B, even you don't fully get all of my layers. Even you, my friend."

"Shut it," John B tells him. "I know you like the back of my hand."

"You see that really big star right there?" JJ says, pointing up high.

We all mumble some variation of "yeah," even though we don't know which star exactly he's referring to.

JJ says, "I named that star Taco Cat when I was nine."

"Taco Cat?" I say. "Why'd you name it that?"

"I liked that Taco Cat is also Taco Cat spelled backward," JJ says, and laughs.

"That's called a palindrome."

"What did you just call me?" JJ says, looking offended.

Kie explains: "A palindrome is a word or phrase that reads the same backward as forward, like *radar, poop, kayak*."

"Palindromes can also be numbers," I offer. "Also, aibohphobia is the irrational fear of palindromes, but aibohphobia is a palindrome itself!" I laugh a little at that fact.

JJ groans. "It's supposed to be summer break, not Mrs. Walter's English class."

"It doesn't hurt to know a fact or two here and there," I point out.

"I liked it, Pope," Kie reassures me, which puts a smile on my face quick. "Speaking of things that I like, I like my freedom." She pushes herself into a standing position, brushing off the back of her shorts. "So I better get home before my parents take that away forever."

I laugh. "Remember that time your parents took away your phone for a month just because you missed your curfew by, like, five minutes?"

"Don't remind me," she says. "I've never read more books in my life to pass all that time."

"Come on, I'll drive," John B offers, standing up and reaching his arms overhead. Unlike the rest of us, John B only had a sip of sangria. He's changed into an orange tank top so threadbare it's practically see-through, board shorts, and flip-flops.

We pile into John B's van and start the trek to drop off Kie first. The drive to Figure 8, on the other side of the island, is always pretty jarring. Despite Kie being a total Pogue, she lives among the Kooks. The houses that blur past as we get closer and closer to her place remind me of something you'd see on a TV show about rich people. I know it's a sensitive spot for Kie, so we don't bring it up, but I can't help but think about it when we drop her off. Her house is nothing like the Chateau. It's, like, five times the size, with paneled windows, a white picket fence, and more than one level. The backyard at her place makes the backyard at the Chateau look tiny. Rumor has it that it's worth over $7 million. She's one of us, but she doesn't *live* like us. I couldn't ever say anything like that out loud to her, though.

The drive back to the south side of the island—the Cut—is a lot more familiar. The houses don't look as nice or as put together. The cars sitting in the driveways are a little more used and run-down. The streets are bumpier, full of potholes. The sidewalks are more cluttered with junk and trash and stray animals.

But that's what home is for JJ, John B, and me.

* * *

TWO MORNINGS LATER, I WAVE GOODBYE TO MY PARENTS as JJ and John B pull up to my house and I climb into John B's van, lovingly dubbed the Twinkie for reasons I still don't entirely understand.

"Thanks for the ride," I say, tossing each of them a breakfast sandwich, courtesy of my mom. Like my dad, she worries that the Pogues are a bad influence, but I think she worries more that John B and JJ have never had an actual home-cooked meal in their lives.

"No problem," John B says just as JJ says, "It's inhumane to get up this early."

It's not even that early—it's eight a.m. I don't have to be at work till nine, but I like to get there when Dr. Anderson does each morning.

"You've been up for nearly an hour, JJ," John B points out. "He was like a cat scratching at my door, *Please, please, John B, come out and play!*"

"The sun rises early in the OBX," I say. "We're on Eastern Standard Time, but we're miles east of the contiguous United States."

JJ pretends to fall asleep as I rattle off facts, but it's true. Technically, we're on Eastern Standard Time like the rest of the East Coast of the United States, but our island is well east of, say, New York City or Chapel Hill or Tallahassee, all of which share the time zone. So we have earlier sunrises and sunsets. In Chapel Hill, for example, the sun rises at 6:15 and sets at nearly 9:00 p.m. in the summertime, but for us the sun rises before 6:00 a.m. and sets before 8:30.

These are the sort of facts that John B and JJ don't find nearly as interesting as I do.

"Are you done, Professor?" JJ asks, but he's grinning. It's not hard to picture him as a wild tomcat, scratching at John B's door. "Anyway, it wasn't the sun that got me up today. Have you seen the waves this morning? Like I'm gonna sleep through something that glassy."

Glassy means the waves are smooth and clear for surfing. I may not surf as much as John B and JJ and Kie, but I know the lingo.

That's just about the only thing John B and JJ wake up early for. Surfing. And fishing, too. They don't wake up early for work or school, not like Kie and me. (Kie is more of a reluctant early riser, but she's willing to set an alarm, unlike JJ and John B.) But surfing, fishing—John B and JJ will practically bounce out of bed if it means being out on the water.

"Seriously, Pope," John B joins in, "are you sure you want to head indoors on a day like this?" He keeps one hand on the steering wheel and gestures with the other to the scene around us: the marshes and seagrass, the sun already high overhead. John B and JJ are wearing board shorts and flip-flops. I'm wearing long khaki pants and a button-down shirt that Mama ironed for me, sneakers with socks.

"Yeah, man," JJ agrees. "You've spent so little time in the sun this summer that I'm beginning to worry you might have turned into a vampire." He lunges across the van and grabs me, sticking my arm out the window like he's testing whether I'll burst into flames in the sunlight. We wrestle as I pull my arm back into the car. Carefully, I straighten my shirt. I don't want to look like a mess when I get to work.

"Where's Kie?" I ask.

"Sleeping off last night's dinner shift," John B answers.

"At least her job *pays*," JJ moans. "I still can't believe you'd give up summer for a job that doesn't pay you a cent."

John B and JJ aren't wrong, exactly. I haven't seen much sunlight lately. The morgue is in the basement, below the police station. And yes, it's an unpaid internship. I haven't told them that I wrote up an official proposal to present to Dr. Anderson in order to get the job in the first place. The morgue's never had a summer intern before. And I knew that the morgue could get me great specialized experience for my future job. Maybe one day I'll even be a coroner.

"I didn't give up anything!" I insist. "This job is great experience."

JJ rolls his eyes. "Why would anyone want the experience of spending the summer indoors—"

"Shivering in some air-conditioned basement—" John B continues.

"When they could be out on the water, fishing, surfing—" JJ adds.

"And generally having a good time?" John B finishes.

"Did you guys, like, rehearse that or something?" JJ and John B grin, and I know they sort of did. "Anyway, I'd rather be in AC than sweating in the sun all summer long."

"You sound just like a Kook, Pope," JJ says, annoyed, "preferring a creepy old basement to the outdoors."

"I wouldn't exactly use the word *creepy*. *Historical*, maybe."

"Nope," JJ insists. "Creepy. And not because of the dead people, either."

"Why?"

"Because of the cops. You're literally in the basement of a police station."

"It's not like I got to pick where the morgue was built."

"I just don't want you to become a spy for the cops or something, ya know?" JJ says mock pleadingly.

"I don't work for the cops," I say with determination. "I work for the morgue. For Dr. Anderson, to be exact, and she's great and smart."

"Is she hot?" JJ asks.

"Who? Dr. Anderson?"

"Yeah."

"Well, she could be your grandmother, so I can't say that I've thought of her like that," I answer. It's not really true. Dr. A's probably about the same age as my parents, maybe even a little younger. But sometimes exaggerating is the best way to shut JJ up. "You guys don't understand. This job's fascinating. And it's going to look amazing on my college applications next year. Dr. Anderson already promised to write me a letter of recommendation."

"Oh my, a letter of recommendation," John B says with a terrible British accent. "Tallyho, good sir, why didn't you mention that sooner?"

"Yeah, now it makes perfect sense that you'd give up your entire summer!" JJ adds. "I mean, a letter of recommendation is way better than spending the summer with your friends."

"I didn't say it was better," I mumble. "It's just . . . more useful."

JJ and John B play at being offended. How could I suggest that anything is more useful than hanging out with them?

Finally, JJ says, "You know the entire point of summer is to be useless, right? Like, to have actual fun?"

"This job is fun!" I insist. "You have no idea what it's like to wash a fresh dead body—"

The guys start shouting in protest before I can finish. JJ leans his head out the window of the van and pretends to throw up just as John B pulls up beside the police station.

"Never thought I'd visit the station without, you know, a pair of handcuffs around my wrists."

"Very funny," I say as I open the passenger-side door, JJ's head still hanging out the window behind it.

I slam the door shut behind me and race into the office, trying not to shiver as the air-conditioned air envelops me. It's about 30 degrees cooler in the morgue than it is outside. It has to be, considering what's down here.

CHAPTER 3

KIE

THERE'S AN ART TO SURFING. IT TAKES PATIENCE. IT TAKES stillness. It takes skill. You have to pay attention: to the waves, to your board, to your arms and legs and feet and hands. If your mind wanders, even for an instant, it can be the difference between life and death.

The best time to surf, in my opinion, is dawn. No one expects anything of me this early in the morning: The Wreck is still closed, so there are no tables to bus, no Kooks and tourists to attend to. During the school year, the first bell is still hours away. My parents are still asleep, so they can't wax poetic about all the different ways I've disappointed them: embracing Pogue life instead of Kook, having the wrong friends, getting the wrong grades, liking the wrong things.

Nothing's wrong when you're out on the water at dawn.

I paddle out and watch the waves. Up and down, up and down. The rhythm is comforting. I straddle my longboard, the water lapping all around me, cold against cold. I stare at the milky early-morning sun, its warmth

23

radiating over my skin. The whole world fades away. Nothing matters now but my longboard and the blue-green water engulfing my legs beneath me.

My fingers drum against my thighs and I lick my chapped lips, salty with seawater. I watch the water swell all around me. I breathe in time with the waves, up and down, over and over. Summer has the best tides.

Once upon a time, I was terrified of going into the waves like this. I would tremble at the idea of being sucked under the ripples of water and drowning beneath the surface, my body washing up along the sandy bank a week later. But now? I've never felt more confident. It's like I *know* the water; it's an old friend and we're back together again after too long apart. No matter that it's been only a day—I was out here yesterday morning, too—it's already been too long.

Breathe in.

Breathe out.

Breathe in.

Breathe out.

Be one with the waves.

Suddenly my body feels weightless, and it's like I can control the growing waves with my thoughts. That's what it's like to give yourself over to the ocean, to trust the water will do everything in its power to keep you safe.

I lie on my belly on top of my longboard and paddle deeper in. The waves are smooth and glassy—gentle, baby waves. I take one after another, not a wobble in sight. But these aren't the sort of waves that win contests. So I paddle out farther, beyond the break of the waves, waiting for something bigger to come along.

My parents don't know I come out here alone most mornings, weather permitting. They'd never let me come if they knew. No lifeguard on duty, no friends to call 911 if things go (literally) sideways. They wouldn't understand that sometimes I need it to be just me and the water; that's how I work up the nerve to take risks: when no one but the ocean is watching.

Suddenly, I see a bigger wave taking shape. That's my shot. A chance to challenge myself. If I can make it through this wave without falling or suffocating in the water, I just might be ready for the competition.

"I'm gonna do it," I say in an attempt to pump myself up.

I swim toward the whirling wave, fighting against the current with every ounce of strength I've got. My arms feel like they weigh a million pounds. I shout, "Paddle! Paddle! Paddle!" to keep myself going.

And then almost in the blink of an eye, I'm on top of the wave just as it opens up. Before I can take a breath or move wet hair from my face, I jump to my feet, bracing myself to ride this beautiful wave. I balance my body, crouch down low, then straighten, raising my arms in triumph.

I'm doing it. *I'm doing it.* I've mastered this wave, too. Now more than ever, I can see myself winning a competition. I manage to even balance myself on my board with one leg.

I turn in the water, and in the distance, I notice a guy there, cheering for me and clapping. He's watching *me*, which hits me harder each second I think about it.

I take a deep breath so I don't lose focus and go back to riding with both legs. And then I ride the next wave back to shore.

"Man, you crushed that," the guy says, meeting me at the water's edge. My pulse quickens; it's the guy from The Wreck, the one with the floppy hair and light brown eyes who asked me where the bathroom was two days ago.

"Yeah," I manage, startled by his presence this early in the morning on an otherwise empty stretch of beach.

He grins brightly. My ankle is still attached to the leash securing me to my board; I nearly trip, and he catches me. Between the run-in at The Wreck and now this, the guy's going to wonder how I manage to get around at all on my own two feet.

"I'm not usually so clumsy . . ." I begin, but he shrugs.

"Happens to the best of us."

Us? He's wearing board shorts, and I see three surfboards sticking out the back of his car, parked haphazardly next to mine at the edge of the beach. This guy is definitely a surfer, like I thought when I first met him. Suddenly his compliment means a lot more. I wonder if he sees me differently and not just as a waitress with a silly dream, but like an actual surfer with potential.

And he surprises me again by saying, "You took on quite a wave. Impressive."

Impressive?

"You work at that restaurant, right? The Crash?"

"The Wreck," I correct him. "But yes."

"I never got your name the other day. Gabriel," he says, extending a hand for me to shake.

"Kiara." I take his hand. "Kie."

"Nice to meet you, Kiara-Kie." Gabriel's hand is pleasantly cool and wet beneath mine. "So this must be a good spot, huh?"

"What makes you say that?" It is—this is one of my favorite spots on the island to surf. But how can Gabriel tell that from one wave?

"Because you're a local, and local surfers always know the best spots. Back home in Barra da Tijuca, my friends and I know all the best places for paddle surfing."

"Barra da Tijuca?" I echo, knowing I must be mispronouncing the name terribly.

"Near Rio," Gabriel explains. "In Brazil."

"Wow! You're from Brazil? I've heard there's amazing surfing there."

"There is. Not just paddle-in, either. Tow-in, too."

"I've never tow-in surfed," I admit. "There's not really much chance to do it around here."

"There will be this week. People are predicting we'll get some of the biggest waves you've ever had around here." Gabriel grins again, his teeth bright white against his tanned skin. "Think you might take the plunge?"

"I'm thinking about it." I feel my cheeks go hot. "I mean, I'd need to find a partner to tow me in and all that."

"I can help you out," Gabriel offers.

I can't tell if this guy is taking me seriously as a fellow surfer or flirting. I find myself hoping for both.

CHAPTER 4

KIE

SUDDENLY, SOMEONE HOPS OUT OF GABRIEL'S PARKED CAR and lets out a whoop.

"Why didn't you wake me up, man?" Without waiting for an answer, he grabs one of the boards from the back and heads toward the water, diving in.

"That's Cole," Gabriel explains. "He's from California, but we travel together when we can. Cuts costs if we split the room and rental car. He wanted to get up with the sun to scope out local spots with me, but he fell asleep somewhere between the hotel and the beach." Gabriel shakes his head affectionately, like he's talking about a misbehaving puppy.

I watch Cole taking one wave after another. On the water, he doesn't resemble an overgrown puppy in the least. He's tall, thin but muscular, with wavy blond hair that's been bleached by the sunlight.

"I think he's the best surfer I've ever seen," I say breathlessly. Cole glides over the water like an ice-skater. He spins on his board like it's standing still.

"You haven't seen me surf yet," Gabriel says with a grin. "Though I have to admit, I think Cole's the best surfer I've ever seen, too."

The sound of an overlarge engine fills the air, and an enormous pickup truck pulls up behind Gabriel's car.

Gabriel moans. "So much for our secret spot."

Our spot? My cheeks go warm all over again.

Two people exit the car, the first from the driver's side, wearing a suit jacket and long pants, his eyes trained on his cell phone. The second person is a tall boy who bounces out from the passenger side, then pulls a surfboard from the back of the truck. He's not wearing board shorts but the sort of long bathing suit Olympic swimmers wear, skintight like leggings. Somehow the pants, striped with a pattern of hot pink and black, make his muscles even more noticeable than if his legs were bare.

"Darren," Gabriel explains. "He's from California, too. Watch this," Gabriel warns as Darren paddles out. Darren glides through the water like a dolphin. Within seconds, he's dropped in on Cole's wave, nearly colliding with Cole.

"That's so dangerous," I gasp, but behind us, the man in the suit is cheering.

"Alan Thomas." Gabriel nods at the man in the suit. "He's Darren's manager. He loves when Darren pulls shit like that."

"Why?"

"When the cameras are rolling, it means Darren will make it on to all the highlight reels. And more exposure means more attention, which means more endorsement deals."

"Endorsements?" I echo. I picture Darren and his tight pants on the front of a cereal box.

Gabriel shakes his head. "Look at them. Always trying to outdo each other on the water."

I put my hand over my eyes like a visor. Cole and Darren are taking turns wiping out and forcing each other to wipe out. It's hard to tell if this is just two guys trying to prove themselves or if they're actually trying to kill each other. Darren drops in on Cole's wave again, causing Cole to lose his footing. Cole scrambles onto his board and does the same back to Darren.

Gabriel shakes his head. "You know they give awards out for best wipeout every year?"

Awards. Endorsement deals. Brands like Billabong and Quiksilver and Rip Curl flash across my mind's eye. I wonder if any of my recent wipeouts would've caught anyone's attention. Not that I want attention for my mistakes. Still, I picture myself accepting the National Surfer of the Year award. Can't blame a girl for dreaming big.

"Darren and Cole grew up surfing in a lot of the same competitions in Cali," Gabriel continues. "They've been competitive since they were kids. It gets worse every year."

"Why's that?"

"Who really knows? They used to be close friends. Cole was represented by Alan first, and Darren was always jealous. Then Cole fired Alan, and Alan reached out to Darren to represent him. Cole calling Darren a sellout and Darren's embarrassment at being Alan's sloppy seconds made them drift apart. It's a long story and I don't want to bore you with it."

I laugh. "It's okay."

The sound of heavy metal rips through the air. Rafe Cameron drives onto the sand in his expensive Jeep, multiple surfboards hanging out the back. I shake my head as he parks, pulls his t-shirt off, and heads toward the water, board at his side.

Rafe's father, Ward, follows his son from the car onto the beach but stops short of the water's edge. I'm not even sure that he notices Gabriel and me standing here. Instead, he makes a beeline for Alan. I watch him point to Rafe as he skims over the waves. Ward's wearing tan linen shorts and a button-down with the sleeves rolled up. Not quite as formal as Alan's suit—at least he's not wearing a tie—but still, clothes that let everyone know he's not on the beach to get into the water.

I'd heard that Rafe was planning to enter the competition, too. Ward has probably bought Rafe lessons with the best surf instructors money could buy from the time he could walk. He's a decent surfer, but next to Cole and Darren, he looks like a little kid beside giants.

I hope that's not how I'll look next to the pros in a few days. Unlike Rafe, I'm entirely self-taught. Well, mostly. John B and JJ and Pope and I all sort of taught one another.

I can hear my phone from where I left it in the car. I set the alarm as loud as I could to alert me to leave the beach in time for the lunch rush at The Wreck. The other night after my shift, Dad finally agreed to let me take time off to train for the competition, but he threatened to take it back if I'm so much as thirty seconds late.

"I gotta go," I say quickly. I twist my hair with my hands, squeezing out as much seawater as possible.

"So, Kiara-Kie," Gabriel says, "will I see you at the competition?"

"I'll be there," I say with some confidence in my voice.

"Don't wipe out," Gabriel says, and winks.

I hiss. "No way." I try to smile as if wiping out wouldn't bother me, but my tone is more serious than I intend.

"But even if you do, that's okay. It happens to the best surfers, too," Gabriel says, like he's preemptively reassuring me, like he can see the future. "If you don't wipe out once in a while, it just means you're not taking big enough waves, right?"

Gabriel's grin is infectious. "Right," I agree, and I actually almost mean it.

As I head to my car, I overhear Alan on his phone, shouting at someone on the other end about "commissions" and "Darren's cut." It all sounds so official and professional, yet Darren is surfing fifty yards away, blissful on the water while someone else makes deals for him, a legit surfer.

Honestly? That looks like the perfect life to me, minus dropping in on other people's waves.

If I win the contest this week, maybe I can get a manager and a sponsor. My parents would finally get off my back about taking over the restaurant someday—they'd have to see that surfing is a real career after all. I'd get to travel the world like Gabriel and Cole, chasing one wave after another.

Even if it means leaving the other Pogues behind.

CHAPTER 5

POPE

WHEN I FIRST TOLD MY MOM THAT MY DREAM IS TO BE A COR-
oner, she thought I was joking. Surely I wanted to be a doctor (the sort who
deals with live bodies), lawyer, teacher, or businessman—that's what she
wanted for me. When she realized I was serious, she cried. She's always been
the superstitious type, and she was scared for me to work in a morgue, afraid
I would attract spirits or ghosts or just demonic vibes, and that I wouldn't
ever get married, because no one wants to be with a person who works with
dead bodies for a living. Maybe she's right about some of that. Maybe I won't
ever land a girl, and maybe I'll get to the end of my life and realize that working in a morgue brought me bad luck.

Or maybe not. I think the work I want to do is good work, necessary work:
finding out exactly what happened to people to give their families closure;
preparing them for burial so they can be laid to rest. Someone has to do it,
right? Why not me? And as far as superstitions, I work with people, not zom-
bies. Bodies aren't that different after the life goes out of them, at least not
right away.

I walk into the Kildare County morgue. There's a skinny, poorly lit stairwell inside the police station that leads the way down to the basement. Maybe morgues wouldn't have reputations for being creepy and strange if they were aboveground and well lit.

The windowless morgue is divided into two main areas. First, the large area where Dr. A's exams take place, the walls lined by mortuary cabinets. Second, Dr. A's office at the far end of the room, walled off with frosted glass. Overhead, long fluorescent lights buzz and hum. There are also smaller lamps, like the kind you see on TV medical dramas that hover over the operating tables. In the center of the room is a long silver metal mortuary table. A large, unseen air-conditioning unit blasts cool air, keeping the morgue chilly even in the heat of summer. It's never turned off; it runs twenty-four seven, all year round, to maintain the morgue's cool temperature.

One of the coolest things ever is getting to wash a fresh dead body. The eyes aren't yet milky and the skin isn't quite pale yet. When washing a dead body, you always start with washing the person's face, gently closing their eyes before doing so if they're open. Then you wash their hair. For women, you sometimes must use a pair of scissors to trim the ends. For men, you sometimes shave their faces.

Next, you clean their teeth and mouth. If someone has dentures, you don't touch them because they'll be impossible to put back in the mouth if they come out. Then you move to the arms and legs, front and back of the body, gently dabbing the wet washcloth on them. Do this, rinse, and repeat. Treat the body gently, respectfully, just as you would if the person were alive.

"Beautiful work, Pope," Dr. Anderson says, hovering just over my shoulder. Dr. A's wearing a long white lab coat with her name and title embroidered in blue thread above the left pocket—*Dr. Elizabeth Anderson, Kildare County Medical Examiner*—along with latex gloves and goggles. Her brown hair's pulled back in a ponytail like always. She's been the county coroner for over a decade, the first woman to hold the job. I know I obviously have to go to school and get certified, but sometimes I fantasize that Dr. Anderson will hire me full-time at the end of the summer and I'll be Dr. Pope Heyward, just like that.

It's nice to spend time with someone who gets it. John B and JJ play at being grossed out by my job, but gross or not, they think it's weird that this is what I want to do with my life, though at least they don't cry over it like Mom did. I don't think it's actually the dead bodies that turn JJ and John B off so much as the idea of being in a windowless room all day every day.

Dr. Anderson explains that the family of Mrs. Jones—that's the body I've been cleaning—believes she died of a heart attack based on recent health issues. "She was found early this morning in her bed, at her home in Figure 8," Dr. Anderson says, reading the record out loud to me from a manila file.

Figure 8 means Mrs. Jones is a Kook. That's the thing about working here, I work on Pogues *and* Kooks. It's the only time my hands will touch a Kook, I swear. Kook bodies are always a bit better maintained than the Pogue bodies that come through here, and usually they're a few years older. Pogues come in with blunt force trauma and other pretty gruesome ways to die. That tells you everything you need to know about living on this island.

"Mrs. Jones has been sent to us to confirm cause of death before burial, since she was alone when she died." Dr. A looks up from the file. "What are the signs that a patient has had a heart attack?"

Dr. A always refers to our subjects as "patients." She says it's more respectful than calling them "bodies."

"Limited blood supply to cardiac tissues results in the tissue eventually dying off, called necrosis. Performing an autopsy will allow a coroner to see this necrotic, or ischemic, tissue," I recite.

"What else should we look for?"

"An enlarged heart, dilation of the chambers of the heart, and breakdown of the vessels supplying blood to the heart."

"And?"

I pause, searching my brain for the answer. "And a characteristic blood clot found in the coronary arteries."

"Ding, ding, ding!" Dr. Anderson trills, like I've just won a game show. "Now tell me, Pope: Should I perform an autopsy to look for any of those indicators?"

Dr. Anderson hands me the file full of Mrs. Jones's medical history. I furrow my brow as I read. Most people think that you need to do an autopsy to determine a person's cause of death, but it's not usually necessary, unless the death was sudden or suspicious. But you still have to play detective to figure out what happened to someone. My eyes move rapidly over Mrs. Jones's file as I read. "Mrs. Jones was seventy-seven years old. She'd been largely immobile for the past year of her life, following a bad fall."

Dr. Anderson nods. "She broke her left hip and wrist."

"She had high cholesterol and a bad result in her last echocardiogram." I keep reading. "Her daughter, Becky Jones, discovered her mother's dead body when she brought her breakfast this morning." I look up from the file suddenly. "How awful."

"It is terrible," she agrees. "But that doesn't answer my question. Should I perform an autopsy?"

Dr. Anderson says that in this line of work, we can't let our emotions get in the way of our logic.

"No," I answer finally, trying not to sound disappointed. "Her medical history is enough to determine that myocardial infarction was the cause of death. Without a specific request from the family, no autopsy is necessary."

"Exactly, Pope. Good work."

I beam under Dr. Anderson's praise. She didn't have to take time away from her day to go over all those details with me—she could've just looked at Mrs. Jones's file and come to the same conclusion I did a whole lot faster. But

Dr. Anderson has been generous with her time since my first day of work. I'm lucky to have someone like her to mentor me.

The teachers at school aren't anything like this. If they were, even John B and JJ might show up to class once in a while.

Actually, probably not.

CHAPTER 6

KIE

THE NEXT DAY, I'M TAKING ORDERS AT THE WRECK AGAIN. THE restaurant is wall to wall with out-of-towners here for the competition. I recognize a few surfers from highlights I've seen online.

I wish I were sitting *with* them instead of serving them. I want to shout, *I'm a surfer, too!* I should be mingling with all these people, talking to them about surfing and trash-talking them about how I want to kick their ass.

"Kiara!" Dad shouts from the kitchen. "Order up for table six!"

"On it!" I say, loading my tray with fried oysters.

Out on the deck overlooking the water, I recognize the pair of surfers at table six immediately. Well, one surfer and one manager. It's hard to miss Alan. He's the only person at The Wreck with a sports jacket on. At least this time it's not a suit; today he's wearing a navy jacket, white button-down shirt, and long khaki pants. Darren's sitting beside him in shorts and a Billabong hoodie.

"Here are your fried oysters," I say with a flourish as I set them down. I smile at Darren. "I saw you on the water yesterday. Those were some serious moves."

Darren doesn't seem to notice my compliment. Instead he says, "I ordered raw oysters, not fried."

"Oh, I'm sorry," I say, remembering Dad telling me how to respond to customers. "We were changing shifts and my coworker must've—"

"Way to blame someone else for your mistake," Darren scoffs.

"I wasn't blaming anyone. I was just trying to explain—"

"I don't need an explanation. I need a dozen raw oysters."

"Coming right up," I promise through gritted teeth, reaching for the basket of fried oysters.

"What are you doing?" Darren says. Alan hasn't looked up from his phone for this entire exchange. Guess there's no chance he might recognize me as the girl from the beach yesterday. "At least leave them here so I have a snack while I wait for the food I actually ordered."

I turn my back before rolling my eyes, my heart beating hard in my chest, fists curled up at my sides. What a douche. It's customers like him that make me want to forget everything Dad says about the customer always being right and just let him have it. But I take a deep breath behind the counter. I'm willing to bet that Darren did ask for fried oysters, he's just scamming for free food. And why bother, when he has all those endorsement deals lined up? There's no reason for him to be so cheap. Then again, Kooks pull this kind of stuff all the time. Some of the worst tips I've ever gotten have been from some of the richest customers.

I see Ward and Rafe Cameron saunter in and join Darren and Alan's table. By the time I bring Alan and Darren their (raw) oysters, Ward is deep into his pitch for Alan to take on Rafe as a client.

I try to listen in. I gotta admit, I'm jealous. As much as I dislike the Camerons—I don't know Ward and Rafe as well as I know Sarah, Rafe's younger sister, but if she's any indication, then the rest of the family stinks—it must be nice to have a parent who supports your dreams. Ward could be doing anything else right now, but instead he arranged a meeting with a sports manager to help make Rafe's dreams become a reality.

My parents would never do that for me. They dismiss my dreams as hobbies, my friends as losers. The thought knocks the wind out of me for a moment, but then I think how that will make it all the sweeter one day when I make it, when I find a manager on my own because of my talent, not because of how rich my family is. I want it to be because I *earned* it, not because my parents bought it for me.

Just then Sarah walks into the restaurant with her boyfriend, Topper, at her heels. I haven't seen or talked to Sarah in weeks—months even—and now I have to serve her fried clams. Her eyes meet mine but dart away quickly. She makes a face like she smells something fishy, and I have to swallow the urge to remind her that she's literally in a seafood restaurant. I hope that I don't have to serve her and exhale in relief as she and Topper sit in someone else's section. Then again, if they'd been in my section, I could've served her spoiled clams to teach her a lesson.

"What are you doing, Kiara?" Dad asks, startling me. "You're staring into space when you've got tables to serve and bus."

"Sorry," I reply, pressing my fingers to my temples. "There's a lot going on this week."

"This place isn't a *hobby*, Kiara," he says, and even though he didn't actually say the word *surfing*, I know he means that surfing is a hobby and The Wreck is a job. "Customers are how we survive on this island."

"I know, I know."

"Okay, then go greet table eight."

"Aye aye," I say, making a mock salute and clicking my heels together like a soldier at attention.

I'm so in my head that I don't notice who's sitting at table eight until I pull out my pad to take their order. Table eight's out on the deck, too—most of The Wreck's seating is outdoors—with an umbrella overhead so the customers are shielded from the sun.

"If it isn't Kiara-Kie."

Gabriel. Cole, the best surfer I ever saw, sitting right next to him. And Allison Kahale, a Hawaiian surfer I've never met but recognize from her highlight reels online. Her thick dark hair is pulled into a ponytail at the nape of her neck, and she's wearing a one-piece swimsuit with a button-down shirt as a cover-up, all but one button undone.

"Hey," I say. Is it just me, or did the temperature on the deck just shoot up by about 50 degrees?

"You're doing a good job, being a waitress and all."

"Yeah, well, thanks." I roll my pencil in my right hand. "It's not what I want to do forever, trust me." I wonder if Gabriel's mentally rescinding his offer to teach me to tow-in surf, now that he's seen how much time I spend at the restaurant, taking orders and getting beer and sweet tea spilled all over my apron, and not on the water, chasing waves like him.

"How long have you been working here?"

"Since I could walk," I answer, which just makes Gabriel look confused. "Sorry, I meant that my parents own this place, so they've made me work here on and off for years. You know, understanding the value of a dollar and all that."

Gabriel laughs, and I worry that I've said something absurd, but he says, "Me, too! I mean, my parents own a restaurant back home. They had me waiting tables from the time I could write down an order."

I smile. "So you know what it's like?"

"Oh my god, yeah." Gabriel grins. "I can't tell you how many nights I came home smelling more like farofa than human." Gabriel looks almost wistful, like he *misses* the restaurant. I can't imagine missing The Wreck. "It's kind of a perfect gig, huh?"

I can't hide the surprise on my face. There are a lot of words I've come up with to describe this job, and not one of them is *perfect*.

"You wait tables for lunch and dinner, leaving mornings free for the water, right? And you make enough money for wetsuits and wax in the meantime."

I smile slowly. I never thought of it that way, but Gabriel is right. If I had an internship like Pope, I'd never have time to surf in the morning.

"Hey, Cole," Gabriel says, turning to his friend. "This is Kie. She was on the beach yesterday."

"I saw you on the water," I say as I shake his hand. "You're amazing."

Cole grins. "Gabe thinks I take too many risks out there."

"I never said that," Gabriel interrupts.

"Oh, really? What about last winter on the North Shore?"

"All I said was maybe wait to go back into the water after the shark warning went up."

"And all I said was sharks have their part of the ocean, I have mine."

Their banter reminds me of the Pogues. I can't help smiling.

Gabriel adds, "Kie's gonna try tow-in surfing this week."

"Maybe," I jump in. "We'll see."

"Oh man, you've got to," Allison says, longing in her voice as though we're talking about her chance to hit the waves rather than mine. "It's not often there are tow-in-level waves in this part of the world. This week might be your only chance for a long time."

I nod. "I know. I want to try."

Allison nods back enthusiastically. "I'm so psyched to have a chance to tow-in here."

"Really?" I ask. I've seen footage of her surfing in California, Hawaii, Tahiti, and Portugal. After all that, the OBX must seem tame.

"Definitely!" Allison answers. "Think of all the surfers who'll never get a chance to tow-in in this part of the world."

"I hadn't thought about it that way."

"Absolutely," Gabriel chimes in. "I mean, you're probably not going to find the hundred-foot wave here . . ." He trails off wistfully.

All around the world, the best surfers are constantly searching for the elusive hundred-foot wave. It's out there, and maybe someone's already surfed it, we just don't know it yet. But I can tell from Gabriel's voice that he's going to spend his career looking for it.

"But there are plenty of gorgeous waves out there that aren't a hundred feet tall," Gabriel finishes.

I hear a shout—JJ, John B, and Pope are walking in the door. The guys must've picked Pope up after work. They make their way to an empty table. Dad hates when they take tables from actual paying customers, but usually I can get away with sneaking them sodas (or something a little bit stronger, occasionally) and the orders that Kooks send back to the kitchen for being over- or underdone. If only Darren hadn't insisted on keeping his fried oysters.

"I'll be right back to take your order," I promise.

"No rush," Gabriel says with a smile. "Take your time. You're worth the wait."

Again, I can't quite tell if he's flirting with me, but my cheeks grow hot. *They* certainly seem to think this is flirting.

CHAPTER 7

POPE

"WHO ARE THOSE GUYS?" JOHN B ASKS.

"No idea," JJ answers.

JJ and John B picked me up from the morgue and we drove straight to The Wreck for dinner. Well, probably not actual dinner, since we can't afford to eat here, but it's dinnertime, and we're here.

I watch Kie grin as she serves a table full of strangers: two guys and one woman. The woman's in a swimsuit and cover-up; the guys are wearing shorts and t-shirts. All three of them are suntanned and fit. I may not know who they are, but I can tell a few things just by looking at them. "They look like out-of-towners," I remark. In the summer, the island is full of out-of-towners at any given moment.

Though I'm not used to seeing Kie so cozy with them.

I can't help it; seeing Kie smiling like that at someone other than the Pogues makes me clench my jaw. I like Kie. A lot. More than she knows and more than I think I've ever admitted to myself before or said out loud. I know she's out of my league. But the thing is, I think she's out of everyone's league.

Like, I have yet to meet a single person as amazing as she is. At the very least, Kie deserves someone who understands her, someone who knows what makes her tick and what makes her stop ticking. And I'm not sure anyone knows her as well as I do.

But Kiara's the one who instituted the no Pogue-on-Pogue macking policy. She made it very clear that she wasn't interested in any of us guys that way. But I swear sometimes, the way she looks at me . . .

Scientific Question: Can love grow between two friends despite the fact that it's against Pogue policy? And can one Pogue change her mind about a rule she made up before the aforementioned love took root?

Hypothesis: If I confess how much I like Kie, then maybe she will confess the same back.

"How was work today, dear?" JJ asks, making his voice all high-pitched, like he's the stay-at-home wife in a 1950s black-and-white sitcom and I'm the husband, bringing home the bacon.

"Really good," I answer, ignoring his tone as I try to make eye contact with Kie. Doesn't she want to get out of here and hang with us instead of these strangers? Finally, Kie gives a wave and heads in our direction.

"You have to meet these guys," Kie says. "They're here for the contest."

Surfers. I should've known when I saw the way Kie smiled at them. Kie has a million different kinds of smiles, but there's one she saves for when she's catching a wave, and she's been giving these guys *that* smile since we walked in.

It's bad enough that Kie was at the Kook school all year. Now we're going to lose her while she's hypnotized by a bunch of surfers she's never going to see again?

John B and JJ must feel the same way, because in seconds, they're giving Kie a hard time.

"Never seen you that happy to be serving up fish and chips," JJ starts.

"Yeah, you definitely seem to have a new enthusiasm for your work," John B agrees.

"Shut up," Kie says, rolling her eyes. "You guys know how much this contest means to me."

"The contest, sure. We just had no idea how you felt about your fellow competitors." John B winks as though Kie has a crush on the whole table.

"Pope, help me out here," Kie begs. "I'm being serious. Don't embarrass me, please."

Asking me to help means she trusts me. That's something.

"Us, embarrass you?" JJ pretends to be enormously offended.

"Gabriel offered to teach me to tow-in surf! Don't mess that up for me," Kie pleads.

"Which one's Gabriel?" I ask, but now JJ's face is all lit up.

"Really?" he says. He rushes off to the surfers' table without a second thought.

"You should've known better than to dangle that tasty treat, Kie," John B says.

Kie presses the heel of her hand to her forehead. "I forgot he wants to try it as much as I do." She sighs. "C'mon, I'll introduce you."

By the time we make it to the table, JJ's already sitting down, leaning back in his seat like he's known these strangers for years.

"Pope, JJ, John B," Kie says, pointing at each of us in turn. Even absent-minded, Kie's motions are always graceful, like a dancer. "This is Gabriel, Cole, and Allison."

"I hear you're towing in," JJ says.

The one Kie introduced as Cole grins in return. "Yeah, you don't get much of a chance to do that in this part of the world. Though I'm not expecting anything major. Even the big waves around here are pitiful compared with the ones we get back home in Cali."

"Pitiful?" JJ echoes. "Our waves may be smaller than yours, but man, you haven't lived till you've stood up during a hurricane. You don't get those in Cali, do you?"

Within seconds, JJ and Cole are deep in conversation about the best local spots. No one hates Kooks and out-of-towners more than JJ, but Cole earned JJ's trust the minute he made fun of the OBX's waves. JJ will do just about anything to prove that he's just as good a surfer as these guys, even sharing the location of his locals-only beaches.

"Why don't you compete, man?" Cole asks. He can tell JJ knows what he's talking about.

"Don't believe in it," JJ says. "Surfing is about me and the water, not me and the water and a bunch of judges sitting on the sidelines."

"Fair enough," Cole answers. "Though I can't think of a better way to make a living."

"Damn straight," Kie agrees.

"Pope, do you surf?" the dark-haired guy Kie introduced as Gabriel asks.

I shrug. "Not like these guys," I answer quickly. I can't help noticing Gabriel's long legs tucked under the table. He's definitely taller than I am.

"Pope's more of an indoor sort of guy," John B explains. "He's got a summer internship in a morgue."

I expect Gabriel to pull a disgusted face, but instead his eyes widen. "Wow, that sounds interesting. Though I have to admit, I'm more like your friends here. I can't imagine working indoors."

"It's probably in his blood," John B adds. "His dad runs the local seafood shop. Spends his days inside, too." John B's face is almost wistful, and I can tell he's thinking about his own dad, who preferred being on the water just like his son.

Prefers. No reason to think about Big John in the past tense.

"Wait a sec." Gabriel suddenly sits up straight. "The local seafood shop—your dad is Heyward?"

"Yeah," I say, surprised. I'm about to ask how he knows my dad when someone starts shouting. I turn and see that Cole is practically wrapped around another one of The Wreck's customers.

"That's Darren," Kie whispers to me urgently. I can feel the heat of her breath against my neck. "Cole and Darren have been rivals for years."

Kie talks like she's known these guys for more than just a day or two.

Gabriel stands up. "Cut it out, guys!" He plants himself between Cole and Darren, a hand on both their chests, trying to get them to calm down. But they don't, they won't. Within seconds, Darren throws a sucker punch that connects with Cole's face, sending him falling into a bunch of chairs. Gabriel doesn't budge, but JJ runs to get in the middle of the fight. Typical JJ.

Darren lands a jab squarely on JJ's jaw.

JJ hits back so hard that Darren falls to the ground. At once, Rafe Cameron is in JJ's face, screaming at him to leave Darren alone. JJ pulls back his arm to punch Rafe, but this time John B is holding him back, giving Rafe a chance to land a blow to JJ's stomach. JJ doubles over, the wind knocked out of him. John B lets go, preparing to hit Rafe.

"I have to stop him," I say breathlessly, reaching for John B, but in the scuffle, I bump the table, and everyone's drinks go flying. I'm drenched in a combination of lemonade, beer, and tartar sauce.

A loud voice bellows, "What is going on here?"

Kie rushes to her dad, trying to explain. But he takes one look at the Pogues and shouts, "You three. Out."

"Dad!" Kie protests. "It's not their fault. Darren started it!"

"Kiara," her father says in that voice that means business. In a lower voice, he adds, "I'm not about to kick out paying customers before I get rid of your freeloading friends."

"If you kick them out, I'm going with them!" Kie shouts angrily. Her hair falls out of its bun as she gesticulates. "My friends did not start this fight."

"Your *friends*"—he spits out the word *friends* like it tastes bad—"are not welcome at my restaurant, young lady."

"We should go," I whisper to John B. "Don't want to get Kie in trouble."

"Kie's not going to let that go," John B says with a smile. I can't help smiling, too. Kie's loyal to us above all, even above her fancy new surfing friends.

"If they're not welcome here, then I don't want to work here," Kie says, untying her apron and dropping it on the floor.

"Kiara," her father says in a low growl, "you pick that up."

"No way."

Kie's dad must realize the entire restaurant is staring. Everyone already was, after the fight broke out, but now they're staring at Kie and her dad instead of Darren and Cole.

Kie's dad adjusts his expression, putting on a smile. "Sorry about that, folks," he begins. "Everyone's a little bit worked up with the surf contest around the corner. Nothing wrong with a little healthy competition, am I right?"

Across the restaurant, the customers murmur in agreement, though I'm not sure anyone actually agrees.

Kie's dad turns to Alan and Ward: "Of course, your meal will be complimentary," he begins. "And as for everyone else," he says, raising his voice, "one round of drinks, on the house!"

Now the crowd cheers as if they've forgotten all about the fight.

"All right," JJ shouts.

"He didn't mean us, JJ," I point out reasonably.

John B shakes his head. "Come on, let's go."

"Actually, we should get out of here, too." Gabriel leaves a wad of cash on the unsteady table. "C'mon, Cole."

Cole's still panting with rage, but he follows Gabriel out the door. Kie steps on her apron as she follows.

"We'll discuss this at home," her father says. "For now, go cool off with your friends."

Kie shakes her head like she's not going to discuss anything with anyone ever again, least of all her father. JJ, John B, and I follow her off the deck and around to the front of the restaurant, where Gabriel, Allison, and Cole are waiting.

Gabriel turns to us and explains, "Cole and Darren get like this before every competition, though it's been getting worse lately." His tone has a hint of big-brother-like exasperation and worry.

"That guy's a jerk," JJ says. "He had it coming."

"What'd he say to you?" I ask Cole.

"He threatened to drop in on every wave I take all week." Cole shrugs. "He's been like this ever since I dropped my manager, Alan, and he took Darren on instead."

How is it that I'm the only one covered in detritus from the overturned table? I wasn't even *in* the fight like JJ, John B, and Cole. My shirt feels sticky and smells worse. I start to pull it off and feel tartar sauce dripping onto my head.

"Why did you drop Alan?" Kie asks.

"I can do better than him," Cole says.

"Damn straight he can," Gabriel agrees. "Alan's a slimeball."

"Aren't all managers kind of slimy?" I ask, though the only things I know about sports managers and agents come from movies. "I mean, isn't that how they earn the big bucks, or whatever?"

"Nah," Gabriel says. "Alan's the sort of manager who'll do anything to close a deal. He wanted Cole to sign with some company that's responsible for polluting the ocean."

"What a creep! As if I'd ever work with a sponsor who's destroying our sport and the planet!" Cole scoffs, offended. "Alan will do anything for money, which is why I fired him. Everything was more about money with him than surfing. He wasn't the person I thought he was. I'll never work with a manager like him again."

"Darren does," Gabriel reminds him.

"Yeah, but that's just like Darren to go after something I had, even if it means selling his soul."

Clearly Cole and Darren have major beef. I can't imagine ever talking about another Pogue like that—even when we disagree, we still always have each other's backs. What happened between these two must have cut real deep.

"And if I remember correctly," Gabriel continues, "that's how you ended up surfing with a black eye in our last contest."

Cole shrugs. "Still won."

Gabriel grins. "Still won," he agrees.

Kie smiles up at him like he's the prize she's hoping to win this week.

Before I can ask Gabriel how he knows who my dad is, JJ turns to me, holding his nose. "I thought we left the rotten seafood inside."

"Don't call my dad's food rotten," Kiara says, still defensive of her family. She turns to me: "But JJ's right, you smell worse than the kitchen floor. You better get home and wash all that off."

"Right," I agree awkwardly, turning to Gabriel, Cole, and Allison. "Well, it was nice meeting you."

"Good luck with your internship," Gabriel says, and it's hard to dislike him, no matter how Kie was looking at him.

CHAPTER 8

POPE

MAMA'S BREAKFAST IS ONE OF THE BEST PARTS OF THE DAY.

Waffles with butter and syrup. Eggs with salt and pepper. And sardines on the side. We stopped doing bacon or sausage for breakfast meats when I was a kid and started using different kinds of fish and seafood products Pop gets at a discount at the store. And as gross as that might sound, it's one hundred percent . . . not that bad.

"Need you to help out at the store today, son," Pop says as I sit down at our small kitchen table.

"I have work—" I begin, but Pop cuts me off.

"After work," he insists. "We're getting a big shipment later, so I'll need a hand."

Over the years I've learned that my father never really asks me for help; he *tells* me to help him. He's really old-fashioned and direct, which can be hard sometimes, but I'll take old-fashioned and direct over not having him around at all. There have been times when I've had nightmares about John B's dad being around and my dad's the one who is missing, and I wake up every single time in a sweat, because that's not ever something I would want. If there's anything I've learned from JJ, it's that at least my dad loves me. If there's anything I've learned from John B, it's that at least my dad is here.

Sometimes I think Kiara could use a reminder in that department, but I'd never say so.

Now I look at Pop and smile. "Yes, sir. I'll be there then," I say.

"Good," he says, and nods his head, like I'm getting his stamp of approval.

"I'm going to head out, you two," Mama says. She kisses Pop's forehead first before coming over to me to do the same. Her lips are wet and squishy, but she presses her love deep into my skin. "I'll keep dinner warm for you two after your work at the store."

✳ ✳ ✳

LATER, I FIND MYSELF UNLOADING A BOAT OF BOXES FILLED with fish, crab, and other sea creatures that we'll package up for people to buy from the shop. The thing about carrying boxes filled with things that live deep in the water: not only are they heavy, but they also stink. And the smell gets on you and finds a way to seep into your skin. It takes multiple showers to get that fish scent out. Mama bought this special kind of body wash that's supposed to help remove that fishy odor and make you smell more like coconuts and lavender. I used it last night after I peeled off my clothes covered in drinks and sauce from The Wreck. Still, when I went to bed, I swear I could smell someone's spilled beer and cocktail sauce underneath all that lavender.

I count nine boxes that I've had to carry from the boat into the store, which feels like some kind of record, but I've also kind of been training for this for years, ever since I started working at Dad's shop when I was eight years old.

That's something Kie and I have in common: Both of our parents make us work at the family business. The difference is my dad wants me to do something else when I'm grown up. The job I've chosen might not be the career he had in mind, but he's never pressured me to take over the store someday. Kie's parents are determined that Kie will run The Wreck after they retire.

I notice Allison Kahale, one of the surfers from The Wreck last night, driving up in a Jeep with a few other out-of-towners. They all look like surfers, too. Allison seems excited when she sees my dad.

"Told you this is his place, you guys!" She yells back to her friends piled into her Jeep as she parks and hops out. She jogs over to my dad, giving him a high five and then taking a selfie with him while I stare at the unfolding scene, dumbfounded.

Usually if anyone comes into the store and doesn't actually buy something, Dad asks them to leave to make space for paying customers (he and Kie's dad have that in common, too), but today Dad doesn't tell Allison and her friends to get lost. Instead, he returns their high fives and handshakes. Someone even pulls a surfboard from the back of the Jeep and asks Dad to sign it.

Okay, what's going on? First Gabriel knew my dad's name last night, and now surfers are showing up and treating my dad like he's some kind of celebrity.

Scientific Question: Why are surfers gathering around the store to see my dad?

Hypothesis: If surfers are here wanting to see my dad, then there is something I don't know about my dad and surfers.

When I'm finally done lugging boxes into the storeroom, I head out front and ask my dad, "What's up with you and the surfers?"

Pop shakes his head. "Don't know what you're talking about. You know out-of-towners make great customers. I'm just being polite."

"Since when are you polite to customers who don't buy anything?"

Pop makes a face like I'm being ridiculous. "Don't make something out of nothing just to get out of work, Pope."

I give up on needling Pop, grabbing a box cutter and heading to the back to wash all the seafood I just lugged inside. That's one similarity between working at Pop's seafood shop and my internship, I guess: washing dead stuff.

One thing that's important to do before packaging is to inspect all the products to make sure nothing has rotted during the time it took to ship to the shop. You'd be surprised how much we have to throw away because it's rotten or just plain unsellable. Pop really cares about the quality of the products he puts out there. He loves his store a lot. As far as he's concerned, the store's an extension of our family.

Once we get things packaged up and labeled, I'm able to put them out on display. It doesn't take long, and soon enough, I have all our king crab out and ready for people to purchase. I'm organizing some shelving when I hear someone coming into the store. I recognize Darren's manager, Alan—the one Gabriel said is slimy.

"Heyward, long time," Alan says, holding out his hand for Pop to shake. Pop doesn't take it. "Still pissed?" Alan asks with a chuckle. "You always were one to hold a grudge." Alan drops his hand. "Listen, man, I just need some Advil for my boy."

It takes me a second to realize that Alan's "boy" is Darren.

"Darren got into a fight with some locals last night."

Even though Heyward's is technically a seafood shop, my dad stocks other stuff he calls "sundries." Painkillers and Band-Aids, chips and jarred salsa. The sort of things people realize they need when they see them, even though they came in intending to buy crab legs and nothing else.

Alan raises his eyebrows meaningfully. "I think your son was one of them." How did Alan recognize me? Maybe he overheard me telling Gabriel who my dad is. Could be he recognized me; everyone's always saying that Dad and I look alike.

"If my son got into a fight, then your boy started it." I've never heard Pop defend me like that. He rings up the Advil.

Alan reaches into his wallet for a twenty. "Keep the change," he says, even though the bottle is twelve dollars.

"No thank you," Pop says, counting out Alan's change.

"Thanks, my brother."

"I'm not your brother," Pop says firmly. He watches Alan's back as he exits the shop.

This is all just too strange. Even though I hit a wall before with Pop, I decide to try again. "Pop, how do you know these guys? Alan and the other surfers?"

Pop blinks at me and makes a face like I just spoke a foreign language. "What are you talking about, Pope?"

"Like, you didn't even shake his hand when he offered it. I mean, I wouldn't shake his hand, either, but after you were so nice to those surfers, you looked at Alan like at any moment you were gonna bite his head off," I say.

"I don't know what you're talking about" is all he says back, and I don't believe him.

"Pop, come on . . ."

"What kinda mess have you gotten into with that Darren boy, anyway?" Pop says, changing the subject. "What trouble have you been getting into?"

"That's irrelevant right now," I argue.

"It's not irrelevant, boy. You're out there getting in fights and stuff. That seems pretty relevant to me. I'd like to know what you've gotten yourself into, before you end up beaten and lifeless on the side of the road."

I get it. He's right. And I know he just wants me to stay out of trouble. I know his concern is real, but still . . . I can't help but feel like he's trying to distract me from something. I'm smart, but I had to get it from somewhere.

"I didn't start it," I say finally. "Darren lunged at Cole, and JJ got caught in the middle—"

"Of course he did. I don't care whether or not you started it. Why is it that wherever those boys go, trouble follows?"

He's talking about John B and JJ. "I don't know," I answer honestly. But I don't argue, either.

"Let's get home," Pop says finally. "Your mother said she'd keep dinner warm for us. You hungry?"

"Starving." I grin. Remembering all the fish I just lugged into the store, I add, "Let's hope she made anything but seafood."

Sometimes that's the sort of remark that will get Pop riled up, and he'll remind me that I should be grateful for whatever Mama cooked for us. But Pop must be sick of the smell of seafood, too, because tonight he smiles and says, "Lord, let's hope so."

He puts a hand on my back as we walk home—so different from my friends' dads—reassuring and constant.

CHAPTER 9

KIE

I AM A GREAT SURFER, I TELL MYSELF ON A CONTINU-
ous loop.

I am a great surfer, and I know I have what it takes.

Repeating this to myself gives me just the confidence boost I'll need to
win it all.

Even though I'm pumped that this day is finally here, I'm all kinds
of nervous.

The sun is out, the sky is the bluest shade of blue, no clouds whatsoever.
And there's a nice breeze, too, and it's just the right amount that helps you to
not feel like you'll die from heatstroke. For now, the waves are gentle and
calm. Nothing I can't handle. I'm wearing a camouflage-patterned two-piece
swimsuit (I hate the word *bikini*) with a black-and-purple rashguard over it,
twisting my hair on top of my head as I stare at the hordes of people gathering for the competition.

Thinking about getting in the water always fills me with excitement, but
today, there's another emotion mixed in there, so unfamiliar that it takes me a

while to identify it. Dread. I can't stop thinking about how many of the other competitors have so much more experience than I do. Today could open so many doors, really jump-start my surfing career. I wonder if there are reps from different companies in the crowd, scouting for talent. Maybe I can get a sponsorship deal without a manager if I play my cards right and crush it out there.

I shake my head. *Don't think about that,* I tell myself. *This is just another wave, just another beautiful day on the water.*

You've got this.

The dread doesn't dissipate.

"Hey there," I hear a voice say behind me. I swing around to find Gabriel. He's shirtless, wearing board shorts and holding his surfboard. His hair and skin are wet, so I know he's already been testing the waters even though he's not competing in today's paddle-in contest.

I wave at him. "Hey."

"Just wanted to find you and say that I'll be cheering for you," Gabriel says. "I know this means a lot to you. Just don't overthink anything."

"You some kind of mind reader?" I ask. "'Cause all I'm doing is overthinking everything."

Gabriel grins. "Not a mind reader. Just someone who remembers his first contest. And his second. And third . . ."

"It gets easier, right?"

Gabriel shakes his head. "The minute it gets easier is the minute you probably ought to be doing something else."

For some reason that makes me feel better, not worse. Because even some-one like Gabriel gets this feeling—this itchy mix of excitement and dread—before every competition.

I smile and nod. "Thanks."

"I'm wearing my lucky shorts in your honor."

"Lucky shorts, huh?"

"I've never lost while wearing them. Maybe the luck will wear off on you."

"I'd hate to kill their lucky streak."

"Wouldn't want it to be killed by anyone else." Gabriel winks, his dark hair falling over his forehead.

The muscles in my jaw feel so tight. Then I realize it's because I'm smiling so hard. Gabriel makes me blush and feel all warm and fuzzy inside. So now, in addition to the mix of excitement and dread, I have a whole new set of feelings rolling around inside my body.

"What do you plan to do with the money if you win?" Gabriel asks.

I've had so long to think about that, and still, I don't know if I have a solid answer. There's probably a whole list of things I would want to do, but to choose one? That feels impossible.

"I'm torn between donating a lot of it to rebuilding turtle habitats or put-ting it all toward my future, getting off this island, and chasing waves on the other side of the globe. Then again, what good is chasing waves if I'm not taking care of the planet, too? Maybe I can figure out a way to do both."

"I'm sure you could," he says. "That's Cole's plan for when he wins the tow-in competition, anyway, so you're in good company."

"Thanks," I say. "That means a lot." I didn't think it was possible to smile even wider, but somehow I'm grinning even more than before.

I look again at the crowd of people gathering a few feet away. I make out Sarah in the rickety bleachers up the beach. I wonder why she's here. Who could she possibly be rooting for? Damn . . . I forgot all about the fact that Rafe *and* Topper joined this competition. She's here for them, obviously.

I guess part of me hoped that maybe she was here for me.

I'm staring too long, because eventually my eyes lock with hers. She waves. Gabriel waves back, grinning from ear to ear like he already won something.

"Friend of yours?" he asks.

"Not exactly," I answer darkly. "It's complicated."

"She looks nice," Gabriel says, and I think he's taking in her blond hair, the skimpy bathing suit top she's wearing even though she's not here to get into the water.

Oh god, what if Gabriel thinks Sarah's hot or something? Could he *like* her? No way, he doesn't even know her. Then again, he barely knows me, and he gives me the same megawatt smile he's pointing in her direction now.

Maybe that smile doesn't mean what I thought it did.

Maybe he's spent all this time talking to me not because he likes me, but because I'm a fellow surfer.

That's okay. I'd rather he treat me like a fellow surfer than some girl he wants to hook up with. But still, I can't help it—I feel foolish.

I thought maybe he liked me.

I was starting to like *him*.

Dammit, Kie. You know better than to let your guard down like that.

It's okay, I tell myself. *It'll all be okay.*

Anyway, I have more important things to worry about at the moment. My stomach's in knots and it's not because I can't stop picturing Gabriel and Sarah making out.

I shake myself like a puppy. *Focus on the water, Kie. Focus on the waves.*

I notice Pope, JJ, and John B joining the crowd, ready to cheer me on like the world's best friends that they are. I'm nervous as hell, but it's nice knowing there are people—true friends—who are here and have my back. That feels good.

Gabriel taps my shoulder. "Like I said, nerves are normal," he says reassuringly. "They're part of the job. A sign you're doing it right, not the other way around."

"I'm doing it right," I echo.

The competition is divided into heats: two surfers at a time, taking as many waves as they can for an allotted period, so everyone gets the same amount of time on the water. Three different heats have taken place so far, six surfers. Allison Kahale is out there now. I watch her glide over the water like a dolphin.

"I thought Allison was part of the tow-in contest," I say. I didn't think I'd have to compete against her. Now I'm not sure I even have a chance.

"She is," Gabriel explains. "But when she saw the waves today, so glassy and smooth, she said no way was she going to miss out."

I nod, trying not to show how intimidating that is. It sounds as though Allison entered the contest today on a whim, while I've been dreaming about it for weeks.

At once, my name is called through some unseen speaker. It's my turn to get in the water.

"Looks like I gotta go," I say, waving at Gabriel and heading to the water.

"Looks like you do," Gabriel agrees. He heads for the bleachers.

The moment my toes touch the water, chills shoot up my body. They ripple through my back, go down my arms, then shoot up toward my head. This is one of the best feelings in the universe.

I glance back at the stands and at my friends before hopping onto my board. Pope, JJ, and John B are waving and screaming. I can't exactly hear everything they're saying, but I know they're trying to be the loudest they possibly can for me. But I also can't help but notice where Gabriel chose to sit and watch me.

Next to Sarah.

Next to the Kook princess herself.

They're laughing like they're having the time of their lives.

I don't know what's so funny between them, but I hate the feeling that I'm not in on the joke. My fists clench at my side and my breathing picks up a little too heavy.

I suck in my lips and turn back to the waves that are picking up. I close my eyes and reclaim my thoughts, even though I'm regretting everything.

Just breathe.

Just breathe.

Just breathe.

You can do this, Kie.

CHAPTER 10

POPE

THE BEACH IS PACKED. THE COUNTY HAS DONE CENSUS STUD-ies on how much bigger the population of our island is in the summer-time versus the wintertime, between the tourists and the Kooks with their summer homes who come here only during those months. The rest of the year, their beachside mansions sit vacant. In the springtime, gar-deners begin the work of perfecting their landscapes, and housekeep-ers dust the interiors so that by the time the homeowners show up after Memorial Day, it's as though they hadn't abandoned their homes for months and months.

In the wintertime, it's easy to forget just how many people can actually fit on this island, but today's a strong reminder. It's like everyone and their mother decided to come out today. I'm not sure I've ever seen so many Kooks in one place. It's easy to spot a Kook, not just by their clothes, but also by their gleaming new surfboards, as well as by the cars in which they pull up to the beach. Some of them drive shiny pickup trucks, others have cars that are older and beat-up looking—but a different sort of beat up than, say, John B's van. It's like how Kooks will buy jeans already fashionably ripped; they'll pay someone to restore an old car, making sure it still looks old because that's part of its "charm." The parking lot behind the beach is lined with Broncos and Range Rovers from the 1980s and '90s. Only a Kook would prefer an unreliable old car when they can afford a smoothly functioning new one.

John B, JJ, and I find a spot in the front row of the bleachers. Kie's standing next to Gabriel right by the shore, waiting for her name to be called.

"How come Gabriel's allowed out there?" I complain. When we got here, they wouldn't let us onto the beach; we had to sit in the makeshift stands someone erected for the contest.

John B shrugs. "He's a surfer, I guess."

"Yeah, but he's not surfing today. The tow-in portion of the contest isn't until tomorrow." Weather permitting. That's the tricky thing about surf contests: they're subject to the forecast. I think that's part of why I never got as into surfing as the other Pogues. I don't like an activity I can't plan.

Normally, John B would make fun of me for thinking about logistics and rules, but I can tell he's not crazy about the fact that Kie is hanging out with someone else, either.

Just then, we hear Kie's name being called on the loudspeaker. Kie grabs her board and heads into the ocean. I flinch when she hits the water, like I can feel its chill on my skin same as she must feel it on hers.

Kie looks good out there. She has to paddle to get out beyond the break of the waves. I watch her take a deep breath and force her board under the lip of a crashing wave, emerging on the other side of it soaking wet. Kie takes to the water the way she does everything—with a lot of patience, care, and joy. There aren't many people I know who love riding waves as much as Kie does, so seeing her in her element always feels special. I'm glad I get to share this day with her. I just hope she wins. I imagine hugging Kie as she lifts her trophy overhead, telling her how amazing I think she is, celebrating her awesomeness like she deserves.

But then that triumphant image is overtaken by another: Kie being dragged from the water unconscious, her board broken in two. Bad things happen on the water all the time. Most shark attacks occur less than one hundred feet from the shore. Attacks on surfers and swimmers are most common in six to ten feet of water. The water could shift beneath her, tossing her off her board. She could hit her head on something sharp under there—a rock, a shell, a forgotten piece of a boat or ship. She could get hypothermia. A million worst-case scenarios ping-pong around in my thoughts before JJ pokes my side. He has no idea how grateful I am to be distracted.

"You see that?" he asks.

"See what?"

"Who Gabriel's sitting with," JJ says, his voice a little too loud, jerking his thumb over his shoulder. If there's one hard truth about JJ, it is that he's the world's worst whisperer. That man wouldn't be able to whisper to save his life. You put a gun to his head and tell him to whisper something, he's a goner.

"Shh," I admonish, turning slightly to see Gabriel sitting with Sarah a few rows behind us.

"Should we tell him she's got a boyfriend?" JJ asks, still way too loud.

"Maybe he doesn't care," John B says.

"No way," JJ counters, and now he's not even trying to whisper. "Gabriel doesn't seem like the kind of guy who'd hit on a girl with a boyfriend."

"Oh, one conversation with the guy, and you're defending his honor?" I ask, as John B explains, "That's not what I meant. I meant maybe he doesn't care because he's not interested in Sarah. I mean, you guys saw the way he was looking at Kie the other night, didn't you?"

From his voice, I can tell that John B wishes Gabriel were the type of guy who'd hit on a girl with a boyfriend, wishes he were more interested in a Kook princess like Sarah than an awesome Pogue like Kie.

"What does Sarah see in Topper anyway?" John B asks. "He's so . . . vanilla."

"Since when do you care what Sarah Cameron sees in anything?" JJ asks, a hint of mockery in his voice. But there's something else there, too. As though he doesn't like the idea that John B cares what Sarah's thinking about anything.

"I just mean that guy's so basic," John B clarifies. "He's not very unique."

"Nothing can be very unique," I correct. "*Unique* means 'one of a kind.' Something can't be very one of a kind."

John B rolls his eyes. "Well, then Topper is the opposite of unique. You could throw a rock at a Kook party and hit ten guys nearly identical to him."

I'm about to point out that a single throw of a single rock is unlikely to hit ten of anything, but I stop myself.

"He's a decent surfer," JJ says with a shrug. Like Kie, Topper is surfing today. I guess that's why Sarah's here, to cheer him and Rafe on.

John B continues: "Sometimes I forget Topper exists. He has such a forgettable face."

"Yeah, so forgettable that half the Kook girls on the island hooked up with him before he and Sarah got together." JJ laughs. "Nothing's worse than people who know they're hot taking advantage of their hotness."

"Are you just saying that because you're not hot?" John B taunts.

"Nah, I'm hot, but in a different way. Like, I'm hot, but in a Pogue way," JJ explains. "Which is infinitely superior to the Kook kind of hotness. It's more unique, right, Pope?" JJ grins, and I decide not to explain that something can't be *more* unique any more than it can be *very* unique.

"Do you think Gabriel's some kind of player?" I interject. "Like, he's been flirting with Kie for days, and now he's sitting next to Sarah . . ." The truth is, I agree with JJ. Gabriel doesn't seem like that kind of guy. But people aren't always what they seem.

"Good old Pope, looking out for Kie's honor." JJ puts his arm around me and pats my shoulder. I shrug him off.

"Kie can take care of herself," John B says assuredly. "Besides, like JJ said, Gabriel seems like an okay guy."

"Yeah, but if he's been playing Kie—"

"You'll what? Don't know if you've noticed, but Gabriel's a professional athlete."

"I could take him," I mumble.

"The three of us together definitely could," John B says. "Not the most honorable thing, three against one."

"Standing up for a Pogue is honorable no matter what," JJ counters, and John B nods. I clench my jaw. Now I'm not sure if I'm jealous of Gabriel or angry at him. I have to remind myself that he hasn't actually done anything shady yet.

John B gives me a curious look. "I'm not sure I've ever seen you look so angry."

"If you get into a fight with Gabriel and he knocks you out, I'll try to bring you back to life, but if it requires mouth to mouth, I'm sorry, but I think you'll have to stay unconscious," JJ says.

"This conversation is ridiculous," I point out. "We're supposed to be watching Kie, not Gabriel and Sarah."

John B and JJ don't argue with that, and we turn our attention back to the water. Kie paddles hard, catching a wave, but she fumbles and paddles back out, waiting for another try. I glance at the giant digital clock set up next to the stands: She still has fifteen minutes left in her heat.

Occasionally, Kie looks back to shore, but she's too far out for me to tell what she's looking at: Gabriel, the crowd, or the judges. Or maybe she's looking at us.

In my peripheral vision, I notice JJ pull out something from a bag he brought with him. He says, "Anybody want some yogurt?"

"Yogurt?" I look over at him holding a plastic cup.

"It's strawberry," JJ says, like John B and I need a little bit more persuasion.

"Strawberry is my favorite. You don't have to tell me twice," John B says, and takes a huge spoonful of yogurt before making a face of pure disgust. "What the hell is in that?" John B spits it out on the ground, causing some Kook guy sitting near us to flip him off.

JJ looks at the bottom of the yogurt container and reads the date out loud. "It's definitely expired. But I'm hungry, so what choice do I have?" He starts eating it, spoonful after spoonful, like he doesn't have any issues with how it tastes, like it doesn't even faze him.

"You can choose not to eat it," I suggest, but if anything, my words make him take the next spoonful even faster.

"It's okay to eat expired food, Pope. What doesn't kill you makes you stronger."

"Yeah, or gives you food poisoning," I mutter.

Minutes later, John B and JJ start arguing about something, but I'm not getting in the middle of it. I've learned to do that over the years of being friends with them. John B and JJ are super tight and they've known each other since they were little kids, and occasionally . . . well, more often than not, they fight like they're brothers. And like brothers, they always make up. I've never told them this, but sometimes I'm jealous of their friendship.

I look at them for a brief moment, watching them go back and forth with each other about whatever stupid thing they're arguing about, and I can't help but smile. John B and JJ are like magnets that choose whether they attract or repel each other from minute to minute. My eyes make their way back to the water.

Back to Kie.

She's lying flat on her board and paddling harder than I've ever seen her.

"This is it," JJ announces. "She's been waiting for this wave."

JJ understands the water better than anyone I know.

"Paddle!" he shouts. "Paddle, paddle."

There's no way Kie can hear him, but that doesn't stop his shouting. He stands, putting his hands around his mouth as he cheers her on.

Kie presses her hands onto her board and hops so that she's crouching. She lifts her hands and holds them out for balance, then straightens up to stand. Now all three of us are on our feet cheering.

What happens next happens so fast I can't quite make sense of it. Suddenly, her feet are in the air, her head flat against her board.

"Ouch!" JJ shouts.

Then she tumbles off her board and into the water. The crest of the wave crashes on top of her, and she disappears beneath the water.

The crowd erupts into concerned ohs, but I don't hesitate. I run toward the water, John B and JJ at my heels. I keep my gaze focused on Kie's head bobbing up and down in the water. Is she fighting for breath? Another wave crashes down on her head. I'm running as fast as I ever have, like something depends on it.

CHAPTER 11

KIE

I CAN'T BREATHE IS ALL I'M THINKING AS I FIGHT AGAINST THE waves, which feel like the heaviest, strongest things in the world right now. The water jolts me violently from side to side, occasionally pulling me down and tossing me up. I can't find my board and my entire body hurts. My legs hurt, my arms hurt, my chest hurts, my head hurts, but I'm still trying my best to stay afloat, to not let this water win, to not let this be the end of the story for me. I can picture it now, my parents punishing me even in the grave. They'll be sad that I'm dead, but they'll take comfort in the certainty that they were right and I was wrong. I should never have spent all my spare time surfing; I definitely wasn't good enough to make it as a pro.

Water gets in my mouth, causing me to choke and gag and spit up. I'm trying to keep my mouth from going under, but everything's just moving too fast. It's impossible.

I'm fighting to stay at the surface, but I feel like I'm sinking deeper and deeper. I try to take in air in the moments when I bob to the surface, but salt and sand fills my mouth, searing my throat. I continue to wrestle the current, determined to swim back to shore, but nothing works. The choppiness is too much to handle. I try to stay calm. You're not supposed to wear yourself out fighting the current; you're supposed to let it drag you backward, away from the beach, or toss you forward to shallow water. You're supposed to conserve your energy, your muscles, your breath. But the messages of *Relax!* and *Don't fight!* that my brain is sending my body don't seem to be reaching their intended destination. I can feel my body panicking, and I can't stop it.

I hear a loud whistle and the sound of an engine in the distance. A minute that feels a lot like eternity passes, and then a lifeguard on a Jet Ski is pulling me onto the raft behind his ski. I grab on to it and allow the lifeguard to pull me to safety back on the shore. There, I'm met with some cheering but also some boos.

I look back at the ocean, my eyesight blurry with salt water. My heat partner's still out there. While I was struggling, the judges stopped the clock, but now that I'm safe onshore, they've started it again. I see her take a wave and ride it smoothly.

"Kie! Kie! Kie! Are you okay?" I hear JJ, John B, and Pope all take turns asking me.

I know I should get up, reassure them that I'm fine. I made it to shore. I'm breathing, I just got the wind knocked out of me. I'm beat up, but nothing's broken. I know I'm fine by the way I can still move, think, hear, and speak.

A tsunami of emotions rushes into me—pain, sadness, fear, and frustration—and it hits hard almost out of nowhere, all at once.

Still, I lie and tell them, "I'm okay. I'm okay." It's what they want to hear.

The truth is I'm the opposite of okay. I blew my first shot. In front of my friends. In front of Gabriel. In front of Sarah and the Kooks from my old school. In front of agents and managers and sponsorship reps from Billabong, Rip Curl, Roxy, and a million other companies that will never want me to work for them now.

"You don't look okay," Pope says to me. "Are you sure?"

There's an ambulance at the ready in the parking lot, a group of EMTs on standby. That's standard at any surf contest.

A medic rushes over to me and tries examining me and asking me questions, but I shrug him off. "I'm fine," I say. "I'm totally fine. I want to try again."

"Ma'am, I don't think that's a good idea," the medic says to me. "It could be dangerous. You may have sustained a mild concussion when you hit your head on your board."

I roll my eyes and lift myself up, annoyed.

Before I know it, I'm crying. I hate crying, but the only thing I hate more than crying is crying in front of other people, especially Pope, John B, and JJ.

"I can't believe this. I can't believe this . . . I can't believe this!" I get louder with each word.

84

My friends pull me into a hug, knowing I need it. Normally, it would work. But the last thing I want right now is to be comforted. I'm too pissed at myself.

"I had one shot, and I . . ." I can't even get the words out, I'm too distraught. I'm shaking. *I blew it. I blew it. I blew it.*

"Kie, you can go back out there no matter what that guy says," John B reminds me. The rules state competitors get a second chance after a wipeout, but all I can think about is wiping out again: the panic, the salt and sand filling my throat, the disappointment.

I'm just too . . . I'm just too broken and shaken up to try again.

"No," I tell John B. "I can't."

"Why can't you?" Pope asks.

"Because," I reply, wiping tears away from my eyes with my rashguard sleeves. Because I'm not good enough. Because I'd rather sit on the sidelines than humiliate myself again.

"We all believe in you. We all know you can do this," Pope says.

I know what he's doing. He's trying to be a good friend, but those kinds of platitudes are the last thing I want to hear right now. Somehow it hurts more than if he'd agreed I'm not good enough. Encouraging and sweet are worse than negative and dour. At least they are right now. I prefer the sound of my parents' voices in my head: I'm not good enough. This is all a waste of time.

"Pope! Enough!" I shout, throwing up my hands so he has to take a few steps away from me. "Just stop! I don't want to go back out there, okay?"

Like Pope, John B and JJ both back up, giving me some space. They've never seen me lose my temper quite like this.

Not only do I feel like a failure, but I also embarrassed myself in front of everyone: Gabriel, my friends, Sarah, Rafe, and people from school. The entire island just saw me royally screw up.

They all saw that my parents are right, surfing is a waste of my time. I'm no better than Rafe, another Kook wannabe who's never going to travel the world surfing professionally.

Just like that, my dream is dead.

Just like that, I'll be stuck at The Wreck forever.

CHAPTER 12

POPE

I DON'T KNOW WHAT I DID TO MAKE KIE BLOW UP LIKE THAT, but I make a mental note that I never want to be on the receiving end of something like that with her ever again. I've seen Kie really upset before, but she's never *shouted* at me. Still, I know Kie and I know myself, so I know the best thing for both of us is to have some space. The best place for me to have that remains the morgue. I had asked for the day off today to watch the contest, but suddenly, I'm longing for the cold air and the quiet buzz of the fluorescents overhead. If I'd been there instead of here, Kie never would've yelled at me. I wouldn't have said the wrong things to her.

After a few minutes of me, John B, and JJ standing around in dumbfounded silence, I wave *see ya later* to John B and JJ and head to the morgue. It's not a short walk from here, but I don't mind. Ever since Kie yelled at me, my heart's been pounding like I'm the one who took a beating on the water. I need the walk to calm down. With each step, I run through every second of what happened at the beach, from the moment Kie took the wave to the moment she went off on me back on dry land. Each time I replay it, I'm confused. I don't know what I said wrong. I told her I believed in her—because I do. I told her to get back out there—because I know what she's capable of. I was trying to help. I was trying to be a good friend.

Scientific Question: Why would one Pogue lose her temper
with another Pogue?
Hypothesis: If Kie yelled at me and not at JJ and John B, is it
because I said the wrong thing while they were saying
the right one?

I shake my head. John B and JJ weren't saying anything at all.

"What can I help with?" I ask as I come up behind Dr. Anderson.

Dr. Anderson looks surprised that I'm here today after all, but when she sees my face, she doesn't ask any questions. I wouldn't have come in on my day off if I didn't absolutely *need* to. Sometimes I think that no one in my whole life understands me quite like Dr. Anderson. Even people like Kie and Gabriel, who aren't disgusted by the career I hope to pursue—they still don't *understand* it.

Dr. Anderson clears her throat. "We just got an unidentified woman from the north side. She's with us until someone claims the body. In the meantime, we can finalize her cause of death."

"Got it," I say.

"Appears to me that it's a gunshot wound to the torso, but we always have to look deeper in case there's more to the story," Dr. Anderson says. I remember her telling me that on my first day working here.

I nod. For the first time since the beach, my heartrate is back to normal. Other people get nervous around dead bodies; I feel calmer. Dr. Anderson pulls on her gloves.

For a while, we work quietly, not saying a word to each other, just focusing on the work. Down here, it's easy to forget what's going on outside; even the climate is different. But then I break the silence.

"Dr. Anderson . . ."

"Yes, Pope?"

"Can I ask you a question?"

"Is the sky blue? Is grass green? Is the sun bright?"

I see what she did there. I smile, appreciating her joke. "Let's say . . . there's this girl who's one of my best friends forever, but this girl entered a surfing competition and wiped out really badly. And then this girl happened to blow up on me out of nowhere."

"This girl sounds . . . complicated," Dr. Anderson says. "Can I get her name?"

"Oh, yeah. It's Kiara, but we call her Kie."

"Kiara. That's such a pretty name," Dr. Anderson says. "So, this girl is one of your best friends, and she blew up at you today when you were there to support her?"

"Yeah."

"I don't think she's angry at you, Pope. Sounds to me like she's angry about what happened—wiping out—and she needed to take her frustration out on someone."

"Why me?"

"Well, if you're really her closest friend, then it *had* to be you. It's the people we're closest to that we know we can blow up at and still be forgiven." She smiles. "My brother has a temper like you wouldn't believe. And when we were kids, I was always on the receiving end of it. But it was never me he was really mad at." She looks up from her work and locks eyes with me. "Do you know what I mean?"

"Yeah," I answer, nodding. "I think I do."

Dr. A looks sympathetic. "*Knowing* it and *feeling* it aren't the same thing, huh?"

"Exactly! Like, I get that she wasn't pissed at me, but it still *feels* like she was."

"And that feels crappy."

I smile. "Yeah, really crappy."

"You know, when I was your age, there was this guy at school. We spent a lot of time together, studied together. We were really good friends for a long time, but then eventually we figured out we had feelings for each other."

"I didn't mean . . ." I scramble to explain. I mean, of course I like Kie that way, who wouldn't? But we have a strict no Pogue-on-Pogue hook-up policy.

Though I'm pretty sure any of us guys would break that policy in a heartbeat if Kie ever gave us the chance.

Dr. Anderson winks. "Just reading between the lines, Pope. You know it's part of the job, playing detective."

She gestures to the open chest cavity in front of us. Maybe someone else would find it weird, having this conversation standing over a dead body, but Dr. Anderson gets it.

"What happened with you guys?" I ask finally. "The guy from high school. Did talking about your feelings ruin your friendship?"

"Sort of. We're not friends anymore." Dr. Anderson grins. "We've been married for twenty years."

I smile back. "So it all worked out?"

"Well, it wasn't magic," Dr. Anderson says. "But I didn't want to live my life full of regret over the chances I didn't take, the things I didn't say. If you live your life with a bunch of regrets, you never really live life."

"Wow, that's pretty deep, Doc. Thanks," I say.

"No problem. And trust that your friend maybe didn't mean to yell at you," she adds. "Wiping out sounds frustrating as all get-out. In the heat of the moment, it's easy to lose your cool on the wrong person."

Before I can say anything else, my pocket vibrates.

My phone's blowing up.

John B: You'll never believe this Pope. Topper just came in second.

John B: I've never seen Kie so pissed.

Me: Who won?

John B: Darren.

JJ: Shit.

JJ: Kie left. If you wanna ditch your zombie-making job and catch some waves with John B and me, we'll be at the beach.

I don't have to ask which spot JJ means. He and John B have one favorite spot, about as far from the competition as they can get without leaving the island. They nicknamed it the Evergreen Bayou because it's so marshy, but JJ says the waves there are the glassiest on the whole island.

Another message from JJ:

Rafe fell almost as soon as he stood on his board. He drove off so fast he left his fancy surfboard behind. 😄 Guess it's my board now, huh?

I reason that it's not really stealing if Rafe abandoned it.

I hand Dr. A the tools she asks for, one after another (scalpel, scissors, forceps). I know I'm lucky to be here with Dr. Anderson. My dream job is right in front of me, so close I can literally touch it. I look at the woman on the table. What were her dreams? Did she get to live any of them before she died?

Today, Kie thought she was getting closer to her dreams, but instead they slipped even further away.

No wonder she lost her temper.

CHAPTER 13

KIE

THE NEXT MORNING, MY BODY FEELS HEAVY AND I'VE GOT A pounding headache that makes me want to scream. The medic may have been right about the concussion after all, but I still could have gone back out there. And I didn't. The sting of disappointment takes my breath away and makes me want to dive back under my covers and never come out.

The air smells like hickory bacon, maple syrup, and French toast. Mom's making my favorite breakfast, and for a second I think she's doing it to make me feel better about how awful yesterday was, until I remember that she doesn't know how awful yesterday was because she and Dad couldn't get away from the restaurant to watch me surf like the rest of the island.

The thought makes my stomach twist so hard I don't think I'll be able to eat an ounce of breakfast.

But then I remind myself that I don't care. Mom and Dad are just two fewer people who watched me humiliate myself. And the fewer people who saw me wipe out, the better.

Anyway, it's not like professional surfers' parents follow them around from one contest to the next, cheering them on like stage parents.

But then I wish they *had* been there yesterday. I allow myself to think that maybe they heard about my wipeout and Mom's cooking something special for me after all, instead of ignoring the fact that I want to be a surfer. I barely slept all night; lying still in bed, I could still feel the waves tossing and turning me. It was like sleeping on a boat on solid ground.

I look at my phone: There are messages in my group chat with the guys and a couple of messages from Gabriel. He says he's never wearing his lucky shorts again, along with a picture of them wadded up in a ball in the corner of his motel room. It's almost enough to make me smile. Then I remember how he sat next to Sarah on the bleachers and how they probably whispered to each other when I wiped out. Maybe they even laughed at me together, but I didn't see it 'cause I was too busy getting wrecked.

It got worse when Topper secured second place and Sarah started celebrating with a bunch of kids from my old school.

Ugh, and the way I yelled at Pope! Nothing that happened was his fault, but I took it out on him anyway.

I pull up Pope's number and draft an apology, but I can't seem to make myself hit send. Why not? It should be easy: *Sorry I acted like what happened yesterday was your fault. I never should've lost my temper. You were just trying to help. Sorry.*

I decide that the least I can do is apologize to Pope face-to-face. He deserves that.

I toss my phone away, telling myself that I'll deal with all of that later. I grab a pillow and put it over my face, pressing it hard onto my mouth. I scream as loud as I can, using the pillow to muffle it all. The scream comes from a place deep within me, and when it's over, I feel a little better.

I put some clothes on and head downstairs to the kitchen. It's gleaming clean; you'd never know that I tracked sand inside last night. Mom told me once that she wants our home kitchen to be a break from all that, a peaceful contrast to the mess in The Wreck kitchen. I mean, it's not *dirty*—Dad wouldn't stand for that—but like most restaurant kitchens, it's busier than a home kitchen, so there's always food out, countless smells, trash cans that need to be emptied, and obviously way more people and chatter.

Mom and Dad are waiting for me, breakfast on the table. They're already fully dressed: Mom in a sundress and sandals, Dad in a black t-shirt emblazoned with The Wreck's logo. The restaurant doesn't open until lunchtime, so breakfast is usually the closest we come to an actual family meal, though Dad often spends most of the time working. Today, he's going over lists of things he needs to order for the restaurant. Mom kisses me on the forehead, and Dad waves without looking up from his work. Sometimes Mom gets mad at him and tells him to be present. Other times, she spends breakfast as focused on her phone as Dad is on his paperwork.

"Good morning, sleepyhead. How'd you sleep?" Mom asks as I sit down at the far end of the table, across from her and Dad.

"Okay," I lie.

"Made you your favorite. It's your half birthday. Figured I could do something a little special."

I should've known better than to think the special meal had anything to do with comforting me after my wipeout. If Mom had heard about it, she'd be celebrating, not commiserating. Because it would mean—as far as she's concerned—that I'm one step closer to giving up my dream of being a professional surfer and settling into the reality of taking over The Wreck someday.

"Thanks, Mom."

I didn't even realize that it was my half birthday. But Mom's parents celebrated birthdays, half birthdays, quarter birthdays. "Any excuse to celebrate," she always says. If I'm being honest, I'm not really big on birthdays. I'm especially not in any mood to celebrate after what happened yesterday. I pick at the food in front of me. I don't have much of an appetite.

I look up and notice Dad squinting at me. "Are you gonna stare at your food or are you gonna eat it?"

Working at a restaurant, I see a lot of food go to waste. Food customers don't eat before it expires, orders they send back, oysters that don't show up as fresh as advertised. Every time Dad has to throw something away, I swear he imagines dollar signs getting trashed.

Personally, it's not the money that bothers me. It's the waste itself. Our oceans are overfarmed, and we don't even sell every piece of fish; people are starving, and we throw away perfectly good meals because the tuna was too well done for some picky tourist.

I take a bite of French toast, pretending to enjoy it as much as I normally would.

"It's really good. Thanks again, Mom," I say. I take a bite of bacon. It gets harder to breathe for a moment. It's moments like this when I wish I weren't their only kid. It might be less pressure if Mom could spread out all those celebrations of hers.

Dad takes a sip of his coffee and goes back to looking at his work. Then, after a few minutes of silence: "We don't think you should surf again."

I stop chewing and nearly throw up in my mouth. "What? Why?"

"It's dangerous, Kiara. I keep telling you that. We heard about what happened out there yesterday. With you getting injured and everything, it doesn't seem like a good idea. You matter more to us alive than dead."

"And you can do so much else with your life, Kiara," Mom chimes in. In the midst of my surprise that they did know about my wipeout after all, I also realize they've planned for this concerted attack. "There's such a big world out there, and you can leave your mark on it in ways that I never could. When I was your age, I wish I had what you have now, but I didn't. And I made decisions that I regret. You have a choice. I just hope you make the right one," Mom concludes, her eyes soft and wet. "How is your head, sweetie? Need an ice pack or Advil?"

"I'm fine. I've taken meds," I mumble. I don't have the energy to say anything else, so I just take a deep breath and ignore everything they said about me quitting surfing. Mom waits for me to say more until, after a few stony moments, she sighs and gets up from the table, taking her dishes to the sink and washing them before coming back. She cups my chin and looks me in the eyes. She runs some fingers through my hair and offers me a warm smile, her dark brown hair framing her face perfectly because she styled it before coming downstairs to cook this morning.

Unlike Mom's, my hair's a mess, pulled into a messy bun at the nape of my neck. I'm wearing a t-shirt and jean shorts so worn in that they're as soft as pajamas.

"You're not my little girl anymore. You're such a young lady," she says, like it's my real birthday.

"Your mother's right, Kiara," Dad says, pushing back from the table, eyeing me up and down. "You're becoming a distinguished young woman. And distinguished young women don't hang out with junkyard dogs."

"What do you mean?" I turn my head, and Mom steps back. I suck in my lips, readying myself for whatever the next insult is that Dad's about to deliver.

"The so-called friends you're always bringing around The Wreck. Troublemakers and freeloaders. You think I didn't notice the Island-tini they swiped the other day?"

I rub my temple. "Dad, they're not junkyard dogs. They're my friends. They mean a lot to me." I've said the words to him so many times it's like I'm reciting them.

He sort of rolls his eyes long and hard. "One day, you'll see how bad they are for you."

I shake my head. "They're not bad for me. Maybe one day *you'll* see *that.*" Even though I'm not shouting, it feels like I have to fight to be heard.

"There's still time to go back to your old school in the fall. All it would take is a phone call to the admissions office."

"No way." Mom and Dad promised I could go to Kildare County High this year.

"What's so bad about that school?" Mom asks. "It's the best private school in the state."

"Nothing good happens there."

"But, honey, you had such good friends there."

When Mom says "good," she means that she and Dad approved of my Kook friends—princes and princesses from Kook Academy—not that they were actually good people.

I shake my head again, swallowing hot spit. "They were terrible friends, Mom."

Dad throws his hands up and walks out of sight, like he's had enough.

Mom leans down and kisses my brow. "I think you should just give it a little more thought. You were barely at the school for a few months before you started begging to go back to public school. Maybe give it another chance?"

I gave it a chance, I think but don't say. I made Kook friends and dressed in Kook clothes and took Kook classes and got Kook grades.

I'd like to say that I hated every second of it, but for a few minutes there, I thought maybe I liked some of those people. One of them at least.

But then it turned out that even the friendliest Kook is still an asshole.

"I made up my mind," I say through gritted teeth.

One thing about my parents: They have this way of looking at me like I'm the biggest disappointment they've ever had. Even if I went back to Kook Academy, I'd find some other way to disappoint them before long. That used to eat away at me on the inside, but over the years, I've learned that what matters more than what they think is what *I* think. What matters more than what they feel is what *I* feel. What matters more than what they want for my life is what *I* want for my life.

Dad comes back to the kitchen, holding an envelope and a piece of paper. "I gotta get these orders into the computer. Could you head to The Wreck for today's deliveries?" he says to me.

I bite my tongue, tempted to remind Dad that if he'd just get Wi-Fi at The Wreck he could do his work anywhere. But I have something else to say that's going to make him even angrier than unsolicited internet advice.

"I'm not working today." Today's the tow-in competition. Even after everything that happened yesterday, I'm not about to miss it. The guys are supposed to pick me up any minute.

"What are you talking about? We gave you yesterday off for the contest."

"Yeah, and today is the next part of the contest. I'm going."

Dad sighs. "Kiara, I'll make a deal with you. You don't have to work at The Wreck for the rest of the summer if you agree to go back to your old school."

"That's not the deal we made." I try to stay calm, but it's all I can do not to scream. "I'm working at The Wreck this summer so I can go back to Kildare County High like we agreed."

"Well, then you better get going. Those deliveries aren't going to unpack themselves."

"I can't go in today!" Now I am yelling.

"Don't raise your voice to me, young lady," Dad says back. He keeps his voice low and calm, which is somehow worse than if he were shouting. "You're going up to The Wreck, and if you don't, you're going back to your old school."

"No, I'm not!" I shout even louder, grabbing my backpack and heading out the door. I pull up my Pogues group chat and text my panic.

How far are you guys?
SOS! SOS! SOS!
Need a ride far, far, far away from my parents.
Hurry! Parents threatening to ruin my life.

I add a row of explosive emojis for emphasis, then dash out of the house, my long hair coming undone from its bun.

"Kiara," Dad calls in that same firm voice, but I don't turn around.

I don't know how to make them understand. I can't go back to that school. I can't be friends with a bunch of Kooks. I can't go in to work today. I can't work at The Wreck for the rest of my life.

I head for the dock, willing John B and JJ to appear with the *Pogue* to head to the tow-in contest like we planned. When I finally see the boat, I wave feverishly and leap on board, not even waiting for John B to kill the motor.

"Let's get out of here!"

"Don't have to tell me twice." John B doesn't ask why. He turns the boat around so fast I lose my balance. JJ catches me before I fall.

When I turn back toward the house, I see Mom and Dad standing on the terrace looking out at the water.

"What's going on?" JJ asks.

"Yeah," John B chimes in. "Why does it feel like we've just assisted in a prison break?"

I'm out of breath, but between sips of air I recount my conversation to JJ and John B. JJ grins. Nothing makes him happier than me rejecting Kook life.

"Hey, where's Pope?" I ask suddenly.

"Where do you think?" JJ rolls his eyes. "He's not about to miss two days of work in a row." He makes the mere idea sound scandalous. I feel a pang of guilt.

"I wanted to talk to him . . ." I begin but trail off without explaining. John B and JJ exchange a look. They saw me yell at him yesterday. "He okay?"

John B shrugs. "You know Pope."

"Yeah," I say, nodding. "I do."

I know that Pope would do just about anything for me. When he saw me getting wrecked yesterday, it was probably all he could do to keep himself from running into the water to save me, and I rewarded that loyalty with cruelty.

"You ready for some tow-in surfing?" JJ asks, eager to change the subject. JJ's not a fan of awkward pauses and heavy emotions.

"Hell yeah!" John B shouts, the *Pogue* picking up speed.

The three of us are silent, enjoying the waves, the pretty blue sky, the sound of water splashing all around us, birds chirping in the distance. I'd rather be on the water with my friends than anywhere else in the world. Even Pope can't argue with that.

If only I'd won the contest yesterday. Then I never would've lost my temper with Pope. Managers like Alan Thomas would be lining up to represent me. I could take off with Gabriel and his friends when they leave the island after the competition, spend the summer chasing one wave after another—on the water, surrounded by friends, all the time, for the rest of my life. I'd be making my own money; I could afford my own place whenever I came back to the island. Mom and Dad wouldn't be able to tell me where to go to school and where to work.

But I blew it, and it's too late to fix it.

CHAPTER 14

POPE

I'M STARING AT MYSELF IN THE BATHROOM MIRROR, TRYING
to shave, when I think about a memory from when I was nine years old. A
really scary storm had rolled in, and rain poured down hard for days. Thunder sounded in loud and piercing blasts, lightning strikes knocked out power
lines, and high winds flipped cars and turned houses inside out. I remember
the power going out as we were watching some Guillermo del Toro movie
that had just been released. Pop went outside to try to fix it, and he disappeared. Seconds passed, then minutes, and he didn't come back. The thunder roared. The lightning lit up the sky.

Eventually, Mama went outside to look for him. I was so scared that she'd
disappear, too, and then I'd be all alone. Mama came rushing back, dragging
Pop's body behind her. I was little then, but I got up to help her drag him
inside, both of us getting soaked in the process.

Pop was unconscious. I thought for a second that he was dead, but then I
saw his chest moving up and down as he breathed. There was a bump on the
back of his head. Mama and I drove him to the hospital, which had a

generator so it hadn't lost power. Pop had a concussion, but other than that, he was okay. It was the first time I'd been in a hospital, unless you count when I was born, which I don't because I can't remember it. I think maybe that was the day I decided I wanted to be a coroner.

Later, Mama told me that she'd found him lying facedown in a puddle. Pop could have drowned right in our yard in a few inches of water. John B's dad disappeared out on the ocean, but sometimes we forget that home can be just as dangerous.

I made a promise to myself that year. My promise was that I would grow up and have everything my family didn't have. There were times before Pop opened up his store when we struggled to find food. There were times when we didn't have running water or electricity. There were times when we didn't have a car or any kind of reliable transportation, so we would walk everywhere. I remember all the kids at school had way more than I did. Hell, there were even times at school when I couldn't afford to eat lunch because I didn't have lunch money. But then Pop opened the store and things got better. And they'll be better still when I finish school and my internship.

I finish shaving and rinse off my face, then rinse out the sink because Mama hates finding stray hairs on the porcelain. Believe it or not, I'd rather think about the time Pop hit his head and almost drowned than about the other memory buzzing around in my brain.

I can't stop seeing Kie's face when she lost her temper yesterday. Her wet

105

hair sticking to her forehead, water dripping off her cheeks like tears. I wonder if she's still upset with me. Even though I know—I think—that I didn't do anything wrong, it still feels like I messed up somehow. Today's the tow-in competition; Kie and John B and JJ are probably out on the water right now, while I'm getting ready for work. Maybe they're even joking about me, the guy who'd rather spend a sunny June day in the basement of the police station than in the ocean.

Scientific Question: Do people stay friends with people with different interests, even if they all grew up together in the same place?

Hypothesis: Common background may not be enough to maintain relationships.

Conclusion: Results pending further investigation.

I toss on my favorite black-and-white button-down and khaki pants that Mama ironed so each leg has a crease down the middle, grab my forest-green engineering club hat, and head for work.

Pop usually beats me out the door, but today he's standing in the driveway, surrounded by *another* gaggle of surfers. I recognize two girls who competed against Kie yesterday and one guy I saw warming up.

Even if I hadn't seen them yesterday, I'd be able to tell they were surfers.

They're in bathing suits with bare feet, their bodies toned and tanned, and they have those tan lines surfers get around their eyes from squinting in the sunlight.

I drum my fingers against my legs, unsure what's happening in front of me. Pop doesn't notice me standing here; neither do the surfers gathered around him. It's like all that matters to them is my dad. Pop shakes his head when someone takes his picture, but he's smiling. For a moment, I seriously consider whether I've ever seen Pop's teeth this much.

I could make a big deal out of this and ask Pop to come clean once and for all about what this is all really about, but I don't have time to stop and investigate right now. I can't be late for work. I make a mental note and file it away for later.

Between Pop and Kie, it feels like work is the only part of my life that makes sense right now.

CHAPTER 15

KIE

I'VE WATCHED ENDLESS VIDEOS OF TOW-IN SURFING. A SURFER stands up on her board, holding on to a towrope attached to the back of a Jet Ski. The ski pulls the surfer onto the crest of a giant wave she could never have gotten to if she were paddling. Sometimes the waves are out in the middle of the ocean or beside hazardous cliffs. Sometimes the water is glassy and clear, sometimes murky and gray. Surfers wear wetsuits instead of board shorts, with floatation vests and helmets. Even when they're surfing in cold water, their feet are bare, because you need your feet to grip the board. I've watched footage of surfers being towed onto waves taller than buildings, coming out the barrel end of a wave miraculously balanced on their board, feats that look so impossible it's like they must've glued their toes in place.

Despite every piece of grainy, water-drenched footage or perfectly clear photograph I've seen, nothing has prepared me for real-life tow-in surfing.

The sun comes out of hiding from behind a few clouds. There's a nice breeze going on, and it's not blazing hot like it's supposed to be the rest of the week, so it's a perfect day to tow-in surf. It's the perfect day to float idly on the water, watching it all, too. One surfer after another is pulled by Jet Ski onto monstrous walls of water, waves that were just suited for paddle-in surfing the day before but, thanks to the changing weather patterns, can accommodate today's tow-in heat and the surfers like Gabriel and Cole who are daring enough to try. Waves try to swallow them, but the surfers conquer them over and over again. It's wild. It's amazing. It's the loudest thing I've ever heard: the cheers of the crowd, the roar of the waves, the engines of the Jet Skis.

I wish I were out there getting a taste of what that all feels like.

One surfer gets utterly pummeled by a wave, the white surf pounding down onto his board so hard that it cracks in half. Jet Skis are deployed to retrieve him, but they have to wait until the water settles before they can get close enough. The surfer pulls himself up onto the ski. He gives a thumbs-up so the crowd knows he's all right. Still, he'll be met with EMTs when he reaches the shore, just in case.

"See, Kie, you're not the only one who totally wiped out," JJ says.

"Remember how I always tell you to think before you open your mouth?" I ask him but also kind of tell him.

"Yes, but remember how I said I think that's total bullshit because you're so anti-censorship?" JJ says.

I roll my eyes. "Totally not the same thing."

"Whatever, Your Royal Highness," JJ says sarcastically. "Whatever will please you and prevent you from saying 'off with his head.'"

John B laughs. "Don't make me turn this boat around," he says in a dad voice. Even though we know John B would never do that, JJ and I keep quiet.

The truth is, JJ has a point. Plenty of people wipe out. This might sound really bad, but seeing that surfer wipe out that hard, cracking his surfboard right in half, makes me feel good, makes me feel less alone, makes me feel less like a failure.

A foghorn blasts, indicating the start of the next heat. I look back at the water and see Gabriel towing in.

"Look!" I shout, but JJ and John B are already looking.

A giant wall of water barrels toward Gabriel, as big as any of the waves we've seen so far today. It takes my breath away. But Gabriel releases the tow-rope and glides down smoothly. As the wave curls over him, he stays on his feet, floating over the spray.

"Holy crap," John B gasps.

"Did I just see him glide down a wave the size of the Great Wall of China like it was nothing?" JJ says.

"Seriously, so sick," John B adds.

"He's truly incredible," I say admiringly.

"Truly incredible," JJ sing-songs, mocking me, but I can tell his heart's not in it. It's hard to make fun of me when he's as impressed by Gabriel as I am.

✳ ✳ ✳

AT THE DOCK, I SEE GABRIEL DRYING OFF WITH A TOWEL. I run toward him, my heart pounding in my chest.

"That was amazing!" I shout. I'm so excited by what I saw that I forget to hesitate, wondering whether Gabriel wants a high five from the girl he watched wipe out yesterday. For all I know, he's hoping Sarah is in the crowd today, cheering him on. I glance around like I think Sarah Cameron is watching, laughing at me because I think that someone as cool as Gabriel is the least bit interested in whether I think he's amazing.

But Gabriel throws his towel over his shoulder and grins. "Kie!" He opens his arms for a warm hug, pulling me in close and tight, and suddenly there are butterflies fluttering around in my stomach.

When we break away, his smile makes me blush.

"I had to congratulate you. I think you scored the biggest wave of the day."

Gabriel shakes his head. "Not even close. But thanks. And I keep my promises—before I leave this island, I'm taking you out on the water for some tow-in practice, if you're still interested."

Still interested? After what I saw today, I'm not sure I've ever been more interested in anything.

But when I speak, my voice comes out sounding shy. "Yeah," I say. "Totally."

"Well, all right then. I'm looking forward to it. It'll be the most fun I've had in a while to teach you some of my tricks," he adds with a wink.

An unseen horn blares to life, causing me to jump. Time for another heat.

"This is Cole's group." Gabriel's voice is flush with excitement. "You think *I* looked good out there? Wait till you see him."

111

Gabriel reaches for my hand and leads me to the stands to watch the competition. We find some open seats and watch Cole's group. But after minutes and minutes go by that start to feel a lot like hours, we're still waiting and there's still no Cole.

"Cole's not out there," Gabriel mutters, standing up.

"He's not competing?"

From the look on Gabriel's face, it's clear that Cole isn't usually MIA on contest days. "No, I mean—so I didn't see him in his bed this morning, and I just assumed that he needed some alone time before the competition started this morning. Cole always needs to clear his head on competition days. It's, like, some kind of ritual for him."

I just nod, listening.

Gabriel continues in a rush: "But now something feels off. Cole would never miss this competition. Not with all the work and preparation he's put into this. I know he might not seem like it, but he takes his job more seriously than anyone else I know."

"What do you mean?" I ask. I think I know what he's trying to tell me, but I need to hear him say it for this to feel real.

His last words send chills up my spine, so I feel hot and cold all at once, like I have a fever. Gabriel grimaces, and for a moment I think he won't get the words out. Then he says:

"I think something has happened to Cole."

CHAPTER 16

KIE

GABRIEL SPENDS THE NEXT HOUR CALLING AND TEXTING COLE, but there's no response. Then he spends the hour after that asking everyone on the dock if they've seen Cole anywhere, holding up his phone with a picture of Cole on the screen. The judges make an announcement over the loudspeaker, calling Cole's name. Every surfer who's not on the water offers to help look, like Gabriel's organizing a giant search party. It's the sort of thing that happens in the movies.

"Don't worry," I offer, even though I know there's nothing I can say that will stop Gabriel from worrying. "This island isn't that big. It's only a matter of time until we find him."

The foghorn blows again, indicating the start of another heat. I see Darren take to the water, having elected to do both the paddle-in and tow-in competitions, where one of the two was good enough for everyone else. A classic Darren move, Gabriel had scoffed when discussing it with me the other day. The guy might be a jerk, but still, I can't deny his talent: It's not just that he catches the biggest wave of the day, but the way he rides it. He glides over the water, making it look easy.

The sky turns from a baby blue to a dull gray. Rain starts as tiny, sporadic pellets, but booming thunder echoes in the distance.

"This isn't going to stay a drizzle," I say.

"We've got to get this search moving," Gabriel insists, and I nod in agreement.

"Hey, man, you can come out with us on the *Pogue*," John B suggests.

"The *Pogue*?" Gabriel asks, holding his hands up like he's shielding himself from rain.

"It's my boat," John B explains. "We can check out all the best surf spots."

Gabriel looks from John B to the gray skies above, then to me.

I nod firmly. "We'll find him." I don't know why I'm promising something I'm not entirely sure I can deliver on.

"Okay," Gabriel agrees. "Let's go."

The four of us—John B, JJ, Gabriel, and I—rush onto the *Pogue*. John B unties it from the dock while JJ stands at the controls, engaging the choke so the engine roars to life.

"That way," Gabriel says, pointing in the direction he wants to check out first. And we're off. JJ's the best one to drive the boat in a storm like this. Out of our circle of friends, he's the best boat driver and he knows a lot about mechanics, so it's easy to trust that he knows what he's doing and knows when we're in trouble.

John B walks over to the other side of the boat and puts his hand on Gabriel's shoulder. "So, what's the plan here?"

"John B . . . we're looking for Cole," I say, like that's not already obvious.

"Yeah, I know, but I think we need to figure out how and where and all that," John B says. He's actually making sense. This is the part where it would be great to have Pope around; he'd pull up a map of the island and come up with a strategic search plan.

"You're right," Gabriel agrees, "but I don't know where to start."

"Let's start at the motel," I suggest. "Maybe he's there now." My voice is full of hope. Gabriel nods, but from the look on his face, I can tell he doesn't believe a word I'm saying. I don't believe them, either.

The motel where Gabriel and the other surfers are staying isn't exactly the nicest, but it's close to the water and has its own dock. It's two stories high. Half its rooms face the ocean, connected by rickety outdoor steps, and the other half face the opposite direction, where there's a grimy pool set into a courtyard, with the parking lot beyond that. Gabriel leaps out of the *Pogue* before John B has a chance to tie off, and I'm close on his heels. We sprint up the dock and up the outdoor stairs of the motel, but when Gabriel opens the door to his and Cole's room, the room is empty.

"Crap!" Gabriel shouts. He looks around aimlessly until his gaze lands on something, and his eyes widen. "Cole's board is gone," he says, then turns and sprints out the door, back down the stairs and back to the *Pogue*.

"Do you know where the naked lady is, just north of here?" Gabriel asks John B breathlessly once he and I are back on board.

"The naked lady?" John B echoes. JJ raises his eyebrows, but I hold up a hand to keep him from cracking a joke.

"There's this place Cole and I went surfing the other day. A beach next to a giant boulder that looks like it had been filed down to look like a naked lady," Gabriel explains. "Cole said it was the perfect place to clear his head. Maybe that's where he went this morning before the competition." Gabriel runs his hands through his hair. "I don't know, man, it's all I can think of."

"Sounds like a plan to me," John B says firmly. I can tell he's trying to sound calm and certain since Gabriel is so frantic.

Gabriel must recognize it, too, because he says, "Thanks, John B."

The rain picks up, turning from a drizzle to a downpour. The water gets choppy so that we're bumping along hard. I sit, grabbing on to the sides of the boat until my knuckles hurt. I've experienced choppy waters before, but I've never been out on the *Pogue* in a storm like John B and JJ have. All I can hope is that as we hit bigger and bigger waves, we don't tip over.

Gabriel sits down beside me. John B's helping JJ, who's doing his best to guide us in between the waves.

Minutes go by and Gabriel remains silent. I build up the courage to check in on him. "Is there anything I can do?"

Gabriel shakes his head. "You're already doing something. You, your friends—helping organize this search."

"We'll do anything we can to help." I feel confident making that promise, not just on my behalf but John B's and JJ's. Pope's, too. "It's okay to be freaking out," I add. Parents and teachers are always saying things like "it's okay not to be okay," but it never feels like they mean it. I actually mean it.

"I'm just . . . I don't know." Gabriel leans forward, resting his elbows on his knees. "I'm worried."

"Of course you are."

"The minute we find Cole, I'm kicking his ass for putting us through this." He laughs, but his heart's not in it. His face dims. "I can't stop picturing every worst-case scenario."

"Try thinking about every *best*-case scenario."

It's getting darker, so I can barely see it, but he smiles a smile that fades quickly.

"Like what?" Gabriel asks. It sounds like he really wants to know.

"Like . . . Cole forgot the competition was today, and he headed out to surf on his own. Or he found out about some even better swell, and he high-tailed it off the island to make it there before anyone else could."

"Or?" Gabriel prompts.

"Or . . . he's out there and needs our help, but we get to him and he's okay."

Gabriel nods, clenching his jaw. John B tosses us each a life jacket.

"Just in case," he says. "JJ thinks the storm's gonna get worse the farther north we go."

"How can he tell?" Gabriel asks.

John B shrugs. "JJ's usually right about this stuff."

"Wait! I think I just saw something," Gabriel shouts, standing. "Quick, find me a flashlight!"

JJ tosses a torch from where he stands at the controls. Gabriel catches it, but when he tries to turn it on, the batteries must be dead, because nothing happens. John B gets his phone out of his pocket and turns on its light, even though it's getting drenched in the rain.

Gabriel points at the water, and John B's light follows, scanning some space on the side of the boat. But there's nothing but choppy water.

"I thought I saw . . . something." Gabriel sounds defeated. "I might just be losing my mind. Sorry."

"No need to apologize," I say.

Gabriel keeps looking out at the water anxiously until we arrive at the beach. But it's empty—there's no trace that anyone was here: not a towel or a surfboard or a footprint. That's the thing about living on an island. At any moment, the ocean can erase every sign of life.

"Where to next?" JJ asks, but Gabriel doesn't have an answer.

CHAPTER 17

POPE

IT'S BEEN EXACTLY FORTY-TWO MINUTES SINCE JOHN B texted that Cole has gone missing. He said that they were out searching on the *Pogue*, but by now the whole island's doing a full town sweep to find him. I don't normally count the minutes until the end of the workday, but I'm paying attention to the clock now because I promised to join the search after work. Whatever happened between Kie and me, and whatever's happening between Kie and Gabriel, *missing* is a big word, a scary word. When people go missing around here, it could be only a matter of time before the word everyone's using to describe them is worse than *missing*. Once I finish up my end-of-day routine—which involves organizing, typing up reports, wiping things down, and handwashing—I rush out the door, waving a cursory goodbye to Dr. A.

"I hope your friend's okay!" she calls as I leave. Of course she's heard the news, too. It's a small island.

I take the stairs up from the basement and see a handful of cops talking on their phones, typing away on computers, drawing maps and graphs on whiteboards. Most people think the police make you wait twenty-four hours before filing a missing person report, but that's an old wives' tale perpetuated by movies and TV shows, based on what police told parents of teenagers who tended to stay with friends and not tell their folks, or wives whose husbands were known to keep a room for . . . emergencies. In reality, you're supposed to report someone missing as soon as you suspect something's happened to them. Because if something *has* happened to them, then time is of the essence.

Every time I come through this area, my chest gets really tight. I'm not sure if it's the fact that they all have guns and sometimes act like they're above the law or what, but fear overtakes me right up to the moment I'm officially out the door and on my way home.

I practice taking deep breaths, looking down at the ground, making sure I avoid eye contact with anyone. That usually works.

Unfortunately, not looking where I'm going also makes me susceptible to collisions, and I almost bump into someone walking through the front doors as I'm about to walk out. I hop to the side to let them pass, noticing that the person I almost collided with was Rafe Cameron, his father at his side. Two cops meet them in the lobby.

"Thanks for coming in," one of the cops says. Ward smiles and nods; he's friendly with the police on the island.

"Whatever we can do to help," Ward answers.

To help with what?

I look back at the door. I'd promised the Pogues I'd help with the search. They're waiting for me to join them. But it can't be a coincidence: two of the island's richest Kooks arriving at the police station, offering to help, the same day a visitor goes missing.

Scientific Question: Is there more to learn outside in the rain or inside the police station?

Hypothesis: If the Camerons' presence in the police station is linked to Cole's disappearance, then more can be learned by sticking around the station to snoop.

My heart thumps faster in my chest as I turn to watch the cops escort Rafe and Ward to an interrogation room near the back. They close the door, which makes things harder, but I walk over to it and bend down like I'm tying my shoes. I may not be able to see them, but I can still hear them clear as day. You'd think interrogation rooms would be soundproof.

"All right. As you know, I'm Detective King, and this is my colleague Detective Wilson. Thanks for coming down for questioning, Rafe."

Rafe is here for questioning. He's under eighteen, which means the police aren't allowed to ask him anything without a parent present.

"I didn't do anything!" Rafe shouts back. "I don't know why I'm here!"

"Let's not get agitated, son," Ward says. "Remember, we're here as a courtesy. It's not as though the police are accusing you of anything . . ." Ward's voice trails off suggestively.

"Of course not," one of the detectives says.

There's silence for a split second. I hear Rafe mumble, "Fine."

"Rafe, we got word that you were with Cole Johnson this morning. Is that true?"

"Yeah. I mean, I wasn't with him. But we were surfing at the same spot." Rafe chuckles, adding, "Don't know how an out-of-towner found it, though. And I'm not sure why he'd want to surf where the water is so green—you can't see all the rocks unless you know where to look."

"What do you mean?"

"I just meant it's a local surf spot. You know, off the beaten path or whatever."

"And you're aware that Cole has since gone missing?"

I can practically hear Rafe shrugging. "Yeah, I heard that, but, like, I saw him this morning. He was out on the water and he was totally fine." Maybe it's just me, but Rafe sounds defensive. Then again, Rafe always sounds defensive, because he's almost always done something shitty to someone.

A cop walks past me, but I don't look up. Luckily, she doesn't try to talk to me.

"Okay, we hear you, Rafe. What were conditions like out there this morning?"

"Uh, the weather was normal. The water was the same as it usually is. I mean, it was a little choppy, but nothing that guy couldn't handle," Rafe explains. "There was no sign a storm was coming tonight."

"So, were you watching him or were you surfing, too?"

"I was surfing."

"Okay. And how was that?"

"Fine, like I said. Nothing we couldn't handle," Rafe says like he's annoyed.

"Did you happen to get angry at any point with Cole during the time you two were surfing?"

"Hey there," Ward breaks in. His voice is still friendly, but there's something simmering underneath it. "Let's not forget that my son is only here to help you all establish a timeline: how long they were surfing, what time he left the beach."

"Of course, but the fuller picture we have, the better," the detective explains. "If your son has any insight into Mr. Johnson's state of mind—"

"I don't know his state of mind," Rafe cuts in. "I just met the guy. It's not like he's missing because of some fight we had on the beach."

"So you and Cole did fight on the beach this morning?"

"I didn't say that."

"But you did fight with him at The Wreck the other day?"

I hear the sound of a chair squeaking against the linoleum floor. "That's enough," Ward says, and his voice doesn't sound so friendly anymore. "My son isn't answering any more questions without a lawyer present. You all should be ashamed of yourselves, questioning an innocent kid like my boy instead of actually going out and searching for Cole Johnson."

This makes me roll my eyes. Kooks love telling other people how to do their jobs, even jobs they know nothing about. Establishing a timeline and Cole's state of mind before he disappeared is just good detective work. There are other people out there searching already. I feel a guilty tug toward the door, the water, my friends.

"Sir, we're just trying to do our jobs. We have a missing boy out there, and your son might've been the last person to see him," one of the detectives explains.

"It's not my son's problem if you all can't do your job on your own," Ward replies.

I hear shuffling in the room, like they're ready to walk out. That's my cue to get up from the ground. I head for the door.

"Not so fast. What are you doing here, kid?" a low, mumbling voice says.

I spin around and am face-to-face with an officer who's bald and has a big, round potbelly and a handlebar mustache. "Um, I'm the intern at the morgue. I'm just finishing my shift, that's all," I say. It's not technically a lie.

"Oh, you're Dr. Anderson's intern, eh? You don't look as smart as she seems to think you are," the officer says. I guess Dr. Anderson's been talking about me. I can't help it, even with this guy sneering at me: I feel proud to know she's been telling them I'm smart. I try not to let it show.

"Um, can I go now? My parents are waiting for me." Another somewhat lie, somewhat truth.

"Yes, but buy yourself some new shoes if they keep coming untied that much," he says. At first I don't understand what he means, but then I remember I was pretending to tie my shoes while I listened to Rafe's interrogation.

I leave the police station and message the group chat that I'm on my way to meet them and that I might have a lead.

CHAPTER 18

POPE

AS SOON AS I STEP FOOT ON THE *POGUE*, I FILL THE OTHERS IN on what I heard. Kie avoids eye contact with me. I can't tell if it's because she's upset about Cole or because things are still awkward between us after what went down yesterday. Maybe both.

"Rafe might have been the last person to see Cole before he went missing, and now he's refusing to talk to the police even though he might know something that would help?" John B asks when I'm finished.

"What do you expect from a Kook like Rafe?" JJ says.

Gabriel paces from one end of the *Pogue* to the other, which isn't very far—the boat's not big. The rain is shifting from a downpour back to a drizzle, but from the look of things, Kie, JJ, John B, and Gabriel have been out here for hours. They're soaked. Within seconds, I am, too.

"We need a new plan," John B says finally.

"Pope, what should we do?" Kie asks. She locks eyes with me, like she really thinks I have the answer. I wish I did.

I press the heel of my hand to my forehead, thinking hard. "Rafe said that he and Cole were someplace off the beaten path. Someplace only locals know. Green water. Rocks that hide under the water."

"The Evergreen Bayou!" JJ shouts. "That's the spot I told Cole about the other day. Had no idea Rafe knew about it." He turns to Gabriel, grinning. "There's no way he could've gotten hurt there. The waves aren't big enough to rough anyone up, especially not someone with skills like Cole."

"Are you sure, JJ?" Kie asks.

"One hundred percent. There've never been waves that serious there. It's kind of a cove, pretty marshy, so the waves can't get that big," JJ explains. "Believe me, I wouldn't have told Cole to go someplace alone if I didn't know it was safe." There's something in JJ's voice I'm not sure I've ever heard before. I realize that he'd feel responsible if anything happened to Cole at the spot he recommended.

I don't have the heart to correct him. The ocean is nothing like solid ground. A place where the waves have never been more than a few feet high can change, depending on the weather. Riptides can appear out of nowhere; sharks can sleep in the shallows. I don't know the water like JJ and John B, but I know that anything can happen on the ocean.

Kie's still looking at me expectantly, like she thinks I'll know the answer the same way I do at school.

"Let's head that way," I suggest finally. "It's the only lead we have."

I expect JJ to argue, but he nods. He hops on the controls, and John B revs the engine.

We get rolling, passing one boat after another. It's like half the island's still helping look for Cole. I haven't seen the island come together like this since the hurricane that came through OBX a couple years ago. We pass boats of people from school, people from parties we've crashed. We pass cops on their boats, too. A bigger boat rolls up by us, and I notice Sarah and her friends on it. They're laughing like they've made some sort of game out of looking for Cole. Ward and Rafe are nowhere to be found. Trolling right behind Sarah and her friends, we see Topper on his family's boat.

"Leave it to Kooks to party at a time like this," JJ scowls.

"Leave it to Sarah Cameron," Kie adds.

John B and JJ assume that whatever went down between Sarah and Kie at KCD this year was typical Kook bad behavior, but I've deduced that it must've been something more than that. Kie's the sort of person who gives everyone the benefit of the doubt, who believes that deep down, no one is beyond redemption. But from the look on her face, I get the idea that Sarah might be the exception.

"How much longer till we get to the Evergreen Bayou, JJ?" Gabriel asks. The rain has finally let up some. It's after seven p.m., but the sky is still light, the sun breaking through the earlier storm clouds.

"It's not far," JJ promises, but Gabriel must've had enough of waiting, because suddenly he puts his hands on either side of his mouth and starts shouting "Cole!" He sounds out of breath, as though he's been running, even though we're all stuck on this tiny boat. "Cole!" He stretches the name out so it sounds like it's about eight syllables long instead of one. If Cole's out there, and if he's conscious, no way he won't hear Gabriel's call. If he's able, he'll start swimming right toward us.

But that's a lot of ifs.

There's some chatter coming through the *Pogue*'s radio, but I can't make out the words over Gabriel's shouts.

"Turn that up!" I call to John B.

John B crawls to the other side of the boat and turns the volume knob to the right. The voice coming out of the radio is still pretty crackly, but we can make out what it's saying.

Authorities say a body has just been discovered washed up bayside near the Morris Island Lighthouse. The body does appear to be that of the recently missing Cole Johnson. No foul play is suspected at this time.

A deep sob rips out of Gabriel on the other side of the boat. He collapses onto the bench beside Kie, crying like he's supplying the world with another ocean. Kie rubs his back in a slow, circular motion. I can tell she doesn't know what to say or do. Tears pool in her eyes. She looks as helpless as I've ever seen her.

"No foul play is suspected," JJ echoes. "That means they think he got roughed up by a wave, right? That he drowned?"

"It could be any number of things—" I begin, but JJ keeps talking.

"I just don't get it. I don't get it. I don't get it." JJ sounds like one of Mama's old records when it starts skipping. "I've surfed there, swam there, fished there, skinny-dipped there—nothing ever happened there." JJ's voice turns desperate. "I didn't think it would be a dangerous place for Cole to be alone. Dammit, dammit, dammit."

"JJ, it's not your fault, man," John B offers.

JJ sniffs and looks up at John B. "I liked Cole. I liked him a lot. I can't believe that he's . . ."

"I know," John B agrees. "I can't believe it, either."

"The waves there were never that big, though," JJ insists. He doesn't sound sad. He sounds *pissed*, which is JJ-speak for sad.

"The ocean can do crazy stuff, JJ," I say sadly. "Riptides can appear out of nowhere, and waves have minds of their own. Anything can happen out there, you know that."

JJ shakes his head. "But you said—you said Rafe said conditions weren't bad!"

"Rafe's an idiot," John B offers.

"And maybe Rafe left before conditions shifted," I suggest.

JJ shakes his head again. "Or maybe it's like the police said. Rafe and Cole got into a fight and—"

"And what, JJ? You think Rafe killed Cole?"

"I think Rafe is a creep capable of just about anything." Now JJ's the one pacing from one side of the boat to the other. "We gotta do something."

"Like what?" John B asks.

"Find Rafe and—"

"You think he's going to tell us something when he wouldn't tell the police anything?" I interject.

"I think we can be a hell of a lot more persuasive," JJ says meaningfully. JJ has a violent side that sometimes frightens me, but I can't blame him for it. We all know he was raised by a violent man. And like I said, angry is JJ-speak for sad. And I'm not sure I've ever seen him this angry, which means he's as sad as he's ever been, too.

"Okay, okay, okay. Just chill," John B says. "This isn't helping anyone." He nods in the direction of Gabriel, slumped in Kie's arms.

We lapse into silence, the only sound the lapping of water against the side of the boat. The ocean is still and smooth now, as if to say, *Who me? I wouldn't hurt a fly.*

CHAPTER 19

KIE

IT TAKES ABOUT AN HOUR IN THE RAIN AND DARKNESS, BUT we finally make it to the Evergreen Bayou. The five of us stay on the boat all night long, not moving, not saying anything. At some point, we all doze off. Early in the morning, John B steers the boat into the shallows so Gabriel and I can swim up to the beach. There's no sign that Cole was here: no towel, no phone left behind on dry land, no rental car parked in the lot.

"He probably hitchhiked," Gabriel admits. "I'm the one who rented the car. Cole hates to drive." Gabriel pauses, and I wonder if he noticed he spoke about Cole in the present tense. "But where's his phone? His flip-flops? His towel?"

"Maybe the police already came and took all that."

"We've been here all night," Gabriel insists. "We'd have seen them on the beach, right?"

"Maybe he didn't bring anything with him," I suggest.

Gabriel shakes his head and paces the beach as though the sand might reveal some clue. But between the rain and the wind overnight, it's impossible to tell the last time anyone was here. Eventually, we swim back out to the *Pogue*. John B drives back to Gabriel's motel. I disembark with him, telling the guys I'll see them later.

Gabriel and I walk up the dock slowly. We slept side by side on John B's boat last night, though sleep feels like a generous word to describe it. More like slipping in and out of consciousness, startling every time a wave moved the boat the slightest bit, as though it were Cole himself bumping into us. I don't believe in ghosts or anything like that—if I did, Pope would lecture me on all the reasons they *can't* exist—but there's no denying that something in Gabriel's face this morning looks haunted.

My whole body hurts, sore from a restless night on a hard surface and still bruised and tender from my wipeout.

The contest seemed like the most important thing in the world a couple days ago. Now it feels like . . . nothing at all. And not just the contest. Everything that happened before Cole died. Fighting with my parents about work and school. Feeling jealous of Sarah because Gabriel happened to sit down next to her. It all seems so small.

I try to think of something, anything, to say to break the silence as Gabriel and I trudge up the dock. Everything seems useless: *I'm so sorry* sounds trite, *Are you okay?* would be a ridiculous question, same with *How are you doing?* or *Is there anything I can do?*

Finally, I try, "Are you hungry? We could get some breakfast." I'm not sure where. The Wreck isn't open yet, and my parents might not exactly welcome us with open arms at home. Not only did I storm off yesterday, but I stayed out all night.

Gabriel shrugs. "I don't know." He stops walking abruptly. "I mean that. I actually *don't know* if I'm hungry or not. That's how numb I feel."

He kicks the ground. His feet are bare and I worry he'll hurt himself, but then I realize that's exactly why he's doing it: to see if it hurts. A tiny bit of blood blossoms over his big toe, but he doesn't even wince. He kicks again and again. Finally, I throw my arms around him, trying to force him to stand still.

"Stop!" I shout. "You could really hurt yourself."

Gabriel laughs as though a broken toe is meaningless. "You know, I'm supposed to leave the island today."

"You are?" Despite everything, I feel a pang at the idea that Gabriel is leaving so soon. Gabriel may be numb, but I'm not.

"Yeah." Gabriel nods. "There's another contest coming up down in Costa Rica. Cole and I were going to—" Gabriel chokes on the last couple of words, like he's just now realizing that he and Cole are never going to go anywhere, never going to do anything, ever again. "Another contest," Gabriel says again. "That's all we do, travel from one waterfront to the next, tracking the weather, chasing the waves. You know you can avoid winter altogether if you travel far enough around the world?"

I nod. I used to imagine myself doing exactly that. There's an old, old movie about surfing called *The Endless Summer.* The title's misleading since some of the biggest waves are winter waves, but I liked the sentiment. The idea that I could chase the weather for the best waves, just like Gabriel and Cole and all the surfers I've spent my whole life admiring. But now, between my wipeout and what happened to Cole, a life on the water doesn't hold the same appeal.

I wonder if John B's felt that way ever since his dad disappeared. I'm not sure I've ever met anyone who loves the ocean more than he does. Well, maybe he's tied with JJ. But I've never asked him whether the ocean lost some of its appeal after Big John went missing. He doesn't act like it, maybe because he hasn't allowed himself to believe that the ocean could've swallowed his father whole. John B thinks he's still out there, alive, biding his time before he comes back home.

"I just don't understand how this could happen," Gabriel says. "Cole was a daredevil, but he wasn't reckless. He's the most skilled surfer I've ever known, and the smartest, too."

Gabriel shifts from the past tense into the present when talking about his best friend, like he needs time to get used to the past tense.

"It's like Pope said," I offer. "The ocean can shift in a second. Riptides, rogue waves, sharks . . ."

"Wouldn't they have said if it looked like he'd been attacked by a shark?" Gabriel asks, referring to the nameless, faceless voice on the radio that told us Cole was dead.

We've reached the back of the motel, a stucco building that might have been white once. There's a pool in front that I know is filled with algae-green water. Guess there's no reason for the motel to keep it in good shape, not when the visitors who stay here come to the island for the ocean, not the pool.

"I know you're right, Kie. Even the most skilled surfers get into trouble on the water. I guess I just never thought it would happen to Cole. I can't make myself believe this really, really happened. Like, I *know* it happened, but I can't *believe* it happened, because it doesn't make any sense."

"It *just* happened, Gabriel," I say. "Maybe you need some time—"

Gabriel throws up his hands in exasperation. "But we'll never know what happened out there, so it'll never make any sense." His breath is ragged, like the lump in his throat is so big he can't breathe.

I imagine Cole's body. What does it look like now? Are there bite marks from a shark up and down his arms? Are his lungs bloated with seawater?

"Pope will make sense of it," I say suddenly.

"Huh?"

"Pope works at the morgue," I explain. "He'll be assisting the coroner with the autopsy." Dr. Anderson—that's the coroner Pope hasn't been able to stop talking about all summer. "They'll get to the bottom of what happened," I promise. "I know it won't make it hurt any less, but at least if you understand what happened . . ."

"Then I'll be able to believe it," Gabriel finishes. I nod solemnly.

"I gotta go," I say suddenly, bouncing on the balls of my feet. "I want to catch Pope before work." This isn't the sort of request you text about. I still owe him an apology for the other day, but there's no time for that now. This is more important. Isn't it? "I'll let you know as soon as I hear anything."

I squeeze Gabriel's arm before I turn in the other direction, snaking my way around the motel. The quickest way to the police station is along roads, not the water.

It's so early that I don't expect to see anyone—the sun's barely overhead—but much to my surprise, there are voices coming from somewhere around the decrepit pool. Probably the building manager, a janitor maybe. I don't feel like greeting anyone "good morning" or having to explain what I'm doing here at this hour, so I crouch behind a row of overgrown seagrass, hoping to avoid being seen.

The voices are coming from people sitting on two of the rusty lounge chairs by the pool. And they don't belong to employees who work here but to two guests: Alan Thomas and Darren.

My first thought is why are they staying at this dump with Gabriel and Cole? Surely all that sponsorship money is good for a Kook hotel. But then I remember that Gabriel said the contest organizers set up lodging for all the competitors, which means they didn't get to choose where they stayed.

"You should be psyched," Alan says. There's an urgency in his voice. "You won the paddle *and* tow-in! You're a champion! Now it's on to the next! Listen, why don't we head to Costa Rica today, get some early practice in before the competition officially begins?"

Just like Gabriel and Cole had planned to do.

I peek around the seagrass just enough to see Darren shaking his head. "There's a body that's just been found, man. Cole's body . . . and I'm jaunting off to Costa Rica to *get some early practice in*? Use your brain, bro." Darren sounds disgusted.

"Calm down," Alan snaps back. "I have a plan."

"No, I don't want to calm down, Alan. Maybe Cole was right when he fired you."

Alan goes silent.

"I just . . . I don't feel like going anywhere yet," Darren says finally, his voice flat.

I shudder involuntarily as I turn away from them. I guess victory isn't quite so sweet when an inconveniently timed dead body is taking all the attention off you. Clearly Darren is more concerned with the optics of his public response to Cole's death than with the fact that his old friend—enemy?—died right here on this island.

What a jerk.

CHAPTER 20

POPE

I'M NEARLY AT THE POLICE STATION WHEN SOMEONE JUMPS
on my back—and not exactly in a playful way. There's something desperate
about the hands clasped beneath my neck.

"Pope!" the person shouts, and I realize that it's Kie. I put my hands over
hers, and she drops back down to the ground, satisfied that she has my full
attention.

"I'm late for work," I say.

"No, you're not," Kie counters. "If anything you're early."

Technically, she's right. But I like to get in early every day, which makes on
time late.

"What's up?" I ask finally.

"Hey," Kie says suddenly, her face softening. "I'm sorry about the other
day, on the beach. I was just so upset, and you were being so nice, and I just—"

"You took out your frustration on me."

"Yeah," Kie admits. "I don't know if I could've done that to anyone else."

Something in her tone makes that sound like a compliment. I think about what Dr. Anderson said, about how we take our frustrations out on the people we're closest to. Is Kie saying—without saying it—that she's closest to *me*?

> *Scientific Question: Just how much can be said without*
> *being said?*
> *Hypothesis: One Pogue can communicate to another with silences*
> *in between the words she says out loud.*
> *Scientific Method: Listen between the lines during every*
> *conversation.*
> *Conclusion: Results pending further investigation.*

So many of my thought experiments end with "results pending."

"Pope?" Kie prompts. She knows I get lost in my thoughts sometimes. She never seems to mind being the one to bring me back.

Her hair is wild around her face, curly from the salt and the rain last night and from sleeping fitfully on the *Pogue*. I stopped at home this morning, had a quick shower, and chugged two cups of coffee before Mama told me it was decaf. Now instead of feeling awake, all I feel is that I have to pee.

"Sorry, spaced out for a second there."

"I can't blame you. After everything that happened, it's hard not to get caught up in your thoughts, huh?"

"Yeah," I agree. Though the truth is I get lost in my thoughts all the time, not just after something happens.

"That's why I'm here," Kie says finally.

I thought she was here to apologize to me about what happened on the beach the other day. Like Cole turning up missing put things in perspective, and she realized that any of us could be gone any minute, so she wanted to make sure she apologized to me while she still could.

Apparently not.

"It's about Gabriel . . ."

Of course it is. I try to shove my jealousy aside. Absurd to envy someone who just lost his best friend.

"He's distraught, you know. I've never seen anyone that upset."

I think about John B, in those rare moments when he lets himself think that maybe his dad isn't coming back after all. He never says so, but sometimes his face sort of glazes over and I know it's what he's thinking. Or JJ, when he shows up at the Chateau with a bloody nose none of us acknowledge but all know he got from his dad.

"I think it would help," Kie continues, "like it would be easier for him to accept what happened, if he knew how Cole died. Like, not just a vague 'on the water' explanation, but the real cause of death. You know what I mean?"

"Yeah, I do," I admit. If I didn't, I'd be going into a different line of work.

For all the detective work and medical know-how, the real reason to become a coroner isn't to solve mysteries but to give people an explanation for what happened to their loved ones. "Kie," I begin, "I'm not allowed to give out information on cases. All the information has to be released to Cole's next of kin first."

"Next of kin means family, right? Gabriel is Cole's family."

"I'm just an intern," I add. "It's not like I'll know anything—"

"Don't give me that false modesty," Kie interjects. "We both know you'll probably figure it out before Dr. Anderson does."

I'm impressed Kie actually remembers Dr. Anderson's name.

Technically, I'm not a doctor, which means technically I'm not bound by the same confidentiality that Dr. Anderson is. Which means I wouldn't technically be breaking any rules if I told Gabriel what I know before the police release it to the public.

"I'll do what I can," I say finally. "I just can't promise it'll be much."

"It will be," Kie says, her eyes wide. "I have faith in you."

✳ ✳ ✳

WHEN I GET DOWN TO THE MORGUE, COLE'S BODY HAS already been laid out on the mortuary table, a sheet draped across his middle, his torso bare. It's not true that dead bodies look like they're sleeping. At least, not all of them. Cole's eyes are slightly open, and I can see the washed-out blue of his irises. His neck is lying at an odd angle, the sort of angle that, if he were alive, he'd roll over to adjust, even in his sleep. His body is bloated with all the seawater it must have taken in.

"What do you think, Pope?"

I don't answer.

"Hey," Dr. Anderson says, her voice softening from her usual businesslike tone. "It's okay if you want to sit this one out. We've never had a patient as young as Mr. Johnson before."

"No," I say firmly. That wouldn't be professional, and anyway, how am I going to get any information for Kie if I sit this one out? I take a step closer to the table, closer to Cole's body. You can still see his tan from all the time he spent in the sun. "Dr. Anderson, look!"

"Yes?"

I point to Cole's neck, where there are faint but distinct red lines.

"What do you think it could have been?" Dr. Anderson asks me.

I examine the length of the lines and how thick they are, the patterns they make around the neck. "It can't be a rope or a noose."

I think for a moment. He was surfing. "I believe that it was a leash."

"Leash?" Dr. Anderson echoes.

"It's a surf term," I explain, "for that strap that attaches a surfer's ankle to their board."

"Oh, of course," Dr. A says with a small chuckle. "You'd think I would know that by now. But I always had my nose buried in a book when my brother and his friends were out on the water." She smiles faintly. What she said kind of reminds me of me. Not that I don't head out there with my friends—I do—but I'm drawn more to my books than I am to the ocean.

"Maybe that's how Cole died," I suggest. "His leash somehow got twisted around his neck." It's not that hard to imagine; I picture the way surfers crouch low as they take a wave. One shift in the water, and Cole could've fallen head over heels, his leash getting caught around his neck as he tossed and turned. I wince. What a terrible way to die.

"Good catch, Pope," Dr. Anderson says. "Although the leash wasn't there when they found his body. Neither was his board. Wouldn't it have been wrapped around his neck if that's how he died?"

"Maybe it snapped off his board somehow," I suggest, "and the end that wasn't secured to Cole's ankle twisted around his neck, and then it drifted away after he died."

My brilliant hunch sounds less and less likely with every word, but Dr. Anderson doesn't dismiss me. Instead, she pulls up the sheet to examine Cole's ankles, adjusting her glasses as she leans down.

"If that was the case, his ankle would be bruised from the pressure of the snapped leash, but his ankle is clean." Dr. Anderson pauses. "What if he didn't have his leash secured to his ankle properly? But then there's that same question: How did it get from the end of his board to his neck?" She steps back, drumming her fingers against her hip. She looks from Cole's ankle to my face. "Don't worry, Pope, we'll get to the bottom of it."

Dr. Anderson's cell phone rings. She pulls it from her pocket.

"Hey," she answers, her voice warm and familiar. Then, "Yeah, I'm at work." Another pause. "My intern," she says, glancing up to smile at me. But just as quickly her smile shifts, and she retreats into her office, closing the door behind her.

Whoever's on the line must've asked if there was anyone here with her, and she answered "my intern." Then the person must have asked for privacy, so Dr. A went into her office so that I couldn't overhear. The walls of her office are glass, but I don't want to be rude, so I turn my back, refixing my eyes on Cole's body like it might reveal its hidden clues.

I hear Dr. A's office door swinging open and turn around.

"Pope, I've got to go," she says breathlessly. "Something . . . *personal* came up."

"Is everything okay?" I ask, then realize it's a stupid question. Of course everything isn't okay. If everything were okay, Dr. A wouldn't be rushing from the office in the middle of an exam. I backtrack, asking instead, "Is there anything I can do to help?"

Dr. Anderson stops. "You're such a good kid, Pope." She smiles. "Please lock up, okay? You can take a half day, head on home. We'll resume Cole's autopsy tomorrow."

Dr. Anderson rushes out the door, so fast she doesn't even stop to pull a sheet over Cole's body.

I know I should just lock up and go, but I can't help it: I linger. Cole's body pulls me toward it like a magnet. I bend over his head, examining the leash marks I discovered. They're faint but unmistakable. I remember Dr. Anderson's voice: "Good catch, Pope."

I pull on my gloves and turn on the bright light that hangs above the mortuary table. Maybe if I look closely enough, I can make another good catch. Some bruise or bump that will reveal what happened to him. I start at his ankles. Like Dr. A said, no bruising from where the leash secured him to his board. I trace my gaze up his legs, torso, arms. On his face there's a shadow of a bruise from the punch Darren threw the other night; his mouth is still slightly swollen. I examine his head, brushing his blond hair aside, looking for signs of head trauma—could he have hit his head on his board, a rock, or some debris under the water?—but there's nothing.

Finally, I pull the sheet back over Cole's body, from his not-bruised ankle all the way up to the red marks on his neck. I check the thermostat, making sure it's set properly so it will stay cold in here overnight. Cole's body needs to be in good condition for Dr. Anderson to resume her exam tomorrow.

CHAPTER 21

KIE

I WENT HOME AFTER I TALKED TO POPE FOR A SHOWER AND A change of clothes, and Mom and Dad were waiting for me with unhappy faces. They threatened to never again let me see the light of day and make me work twenty-four-hour shifts at The Wreck for a whole week. I tried to explain everything about Cole and Gabriel in between their threats, but I don't think they heard me over their disappointment. Luckily, they had to leave for The Wreck before they could land on one punishment or another. Alone, I'm grateful for the quiet of an empty house. No way am I going in to work today. I text our group chat, and we all meet up.

We're back on the *Pogue*—John B, JJ, Gabriel, and me. I don't know why. Cole's body's been found. It's not like we might find him all over again. But what else can we do? The thought of sitting around the Chateau all day makes me itch. We needed to get back on the water, even if there's no good reason to be here.

"Where to?" John B asks.

I shrug. JJ shrugs. Gabriel shrugs. Finally, JJ says, "Just get us out of here." He hunches his shoulders, and I know he's feeling as itchy as I am. I want to *do* something, I want to *go* somewhere. But there's nothing to do. There's nowhere to go.

"It'll be better after Pope gets off work." I don't know if I'm saying it to Gabriel or to myself.

"Yeah," JJ agrees. "Pope will make sense of it."

I nod like I believe him, but the truth is, even if Pope figures out what happened to the most minute detail, I'm not sure Cole's death will ever make sense.

I don't know whether John B intended to drive us back to the Evergreen Bayou, but it seems like I blink and then we're here. The last place Cole was seen alive. It's foggy and the water is still, the waves lapping gently through the marshes.

"Man, I don't want to be here," JJ moans, and John B nods, revving the engine to get us out of here as quickly as possible. But then there's a splash and I turn around. Behind me, Gabriel has leaped from the moving boat into the water.

"Cut the engine!" I shout.

Gabriel swims through the boat's wake, one arm over the other over the other. He's the best swimmer I've ever seen, and that's saying something. He moves through the water so fast that I find myself thinking that if he wasn't a surfer, he probably could've been an Olympic-level swimmer.

"Gabriel, what are you doing?" I call. "Come back!"

"Look!" JJ points to a shadow a few yards in front of Gabriel.

No, not a shadow. A surfboard.

Gabriel gets to the board and throws his arms over it, like he's hugging it hello. Then he starts paddling back to the *Pogue*.

I don't have to ask whose board it is. None of us do. JJ helps Gabriel get it onto the boat, then Gabriel heaves himself up out of the water, too.

We stand there silently for a few minutes, all of us staring at the board. Finally, John B asks, "Should we bring it to the police station? It might help with their investigation."

Gabriel shakes his head, water dripping from the ends of his hair. "Not yet."

As John B finally points the *Pogue* away from the beach, Gabriel keeps one hand on the board, like he can't bear to let it go.

✳ ✳ ✳

BACK AT THE CHATEAU, GABRIEL PLANTS THE BOARD ON THE ground, leaning against a tree. He sits down across from it, gazing at it as though he expects it to say something.

"It's in perfect shape," he says finally. The board is cream-colored with a dark red stripe down the center.

"Yeah," I agree. "It's got kind of a retro California vibe." I didn't get to know Cole that well, but I think it fit his personality.

Gabriel nods.

"I like it."

"Me, too."

In my pocket, my phone buzzes with a text. I know without looking that it's my parents, probably Dad, reminding me that it's the dinner rush and I better *get to work right now or there'll be consequences, young lady.* I bet if I were ditching work to hang out with Sarah Cameron instead of the Pogues he wouldn't mind. He might tell me to never come to work again if I spent my free time hanging out with people my mom and dad think of as the "right" people. Leave it to my parents to have absolutely no perspective even when someone just died.

"Hey!" Pope shouts as he jogs into the backyard, a little out of breath.

Gabriel pops up like he was sitting on a spring. He looks at Pope expectantly. John B tosses a can of cheap beer to Pope, then to me, then to Gabriel. Gabriel opens his and takes a long, slow gulp.

"Well?" he says, wiping his mouth.

"Our initial examination was inconclusive," Pope begins.

"What the hell does that mean?" JJ asks.

"Dr. Anderson had to leave early today—"

"She just left?" I interrupt. "Without completing the—" I can't bring myself to say the word *autopsy.*

"She had some kind of emergency," Pope explains, but I shake my head.

"What kind of emergency could be more important than *this*?" JJ says, asking exactly the question I'm thinking.

"I didn't ask," Pope says. "She said it was personal."

150

"Okay," I say finally, trying to keep my voice calm. I don't want to explode at Pope all over again, no matter how frustrated I am. "But you must have seen something in your *initial examination*." I'm careful to use the same words Pope did. "I mean, aren't there things you can tell just by looking?"

Pope opens his mouth, then closes it, which I know means that there's something he's not telling us.

"Please, man." Gabriel's voice is quieter and much calmer than the rest of ours. "Please," he repeats.

Pope takes a long swig of his beer. "Okay." He takes a deep breath, then sets his gaze like he does when he's made up his mind about something. "There were marks around Cole's neck that suggest he didn't drown."

"What kind of marks?" John B asks.

"I can't say for sure, but it looked like maybe leash marks. I think—and Dr. Anderson didn't disagree—that his leash must have gotten twisted around his neck somehow."

"How?" JJ asks.

But Pope's attention has diverted. "Whose board is that?" he asks suddenly.

"Cole's," I answer. "Gabriel found it today near the Evergreen Bayou."

"You really should submit it to the police."

JJ rolls his eyes. "Always such a stickler for the rules."

"We're going to," I promise, before JJ and Pope can start debating the value of rules. "We just haven't yet."

Pope steps toward the surfboard. "I really shouldn't do this," he says. "It's evidence." He pauses. "But the leash is intact, fastened to the board like it should be."

"Where else would it be?" JJ scoffs. I elbow him in the ribs. I recognize the look on Pope's face. He's not going to let the rules stop him now, because his brain is working something out. And once Pope's brain is working something out, nothing stops him until he's finished, or at least until he tries to finish.

Pope grabs Cole's board and lays it flat on the ground. He stands on the board, strapping the leash to his ankle. He crouches as though he's riding a wave, then tugs the leash. Even in a crouch, it's not long enough to reach his neck.

"No way, man," JJ says.

Pope lies flat on the board and mimics hefting himself onto his feet—but even then, the leash is too short.

"Okay, well, if he fell off the back of his board and doubled over, maybe then?"

"No way the leash would've gotten wrapped around his neck," JJ insists.

Pope quickly jumps down from the board, propping it back up against the tree. He starts pacing back and forth.

"Maybe he didn't have the leash secured to his ankle," he murmurs, and I can tell he's not talking to us but thinking out loud. "And he got thrown from the board and somehow got twisted in the leash, tight enough to strangle him. But then, wouldn't they have found his body with the board, the leash still wrapped around his neck?"

"Maybe it wasn't his leash," JJ suggests. "Maybe someone wrapped *their* leash around Cole's neck."

"But who would want to hurt Cole?" Pope asks. I'm surprised he's taking JJ's theory seriously. But then again, I guess that's Pope's scientific method at work. He has to consider every possibility.

"What about Darren?" JJ suggests. "Just a few days ago, he tried to beat the shit out of Cole. Gabriel said their rivalry had been getting uglier."

"Darren?" I echo, thinking of the conversation I overheard at the motel this morning. I thought he was all riled up because of how much attention Cole's disappearance and death had taken from his big win. But what if he was feeling guilty?

"We have to go to the police," JJ says.

"And tell them what?" John B asks. "We don't have anything that points in Darren's direction."

"Maybe Rafe saw something," Pope offers. "He said that Cole was still alive when he left him yesterday morning, but he didn't say whether anyone else was at the beach that day."

"Okay, but if Rafe saw Darren there, why wouldn't he have said so?" John B asks. "From what you said, Ward got pissed when it sounded like the police were accusing his son of something. If Rafe could've pointed the police in someone else's direction, no way would he have stayed quiet."

"Unless he was lying," I interject. "Think about it: Ward was trying to get Darren's manager to represent Rafe. Ward would never let Rafe say anything that might turn Alan against him—and implicating Alan's star client in a murder is hardly a way to stay on Alan's good side."

Now I'm the one pacing. I finally understand why Pope does this when he's thinking hard. When all these thoughts are racing around your brain, it feels impossible to keep still. It's like you have to keep moving in order to catch them.

"In fact, maybe that's why Rafe told the police he'd been surfing at the Evergreen Bayou to begin with—so that he could specifically say that he hadn't seen Darren there. Maybe Rafe thought that protecting Alan's star client would get Alan to rep him, despite his mediocre surfing skills."

I stop pacing and look up at the guys. No one says anything.

"Well?" I ask. "What do you think?"

John B pulls a face. "It's a little far-fetched, Kie. I mean, Rafe is a creep, but he wouldn't help a murderer just to blackmail someone into being his manager, would he?"

"Of course he would," JJ answers. "Kooks'll do anything to get what they think they deserve. And they think they deserve *everything*."

I look at Gabriel. He hasn't said a word since Pope hopped on Cole's board.

"You know Darren better than the rest of us," I say gently. "Do you think he could've hurt Cole?"

Gabriel closes his eyes. "I know Darren would *hurt* Cole. I've seen him *hurt*

Cole. But kill him?" He opens his eyes and locks his gaze on mine. "I honestly don't know."

"We have to wait," Pope breaks in. "Once the autopsy is complete and the cause of death is ruled strangulation, there will be proof that Cole didn't just drown. The police will call Rafe back in for questioning, and Ward won't be able to storm out this time. Even if Rafe is trying to get Alan to represent him, he won't keep lying for Darren forever. What good will having a manager do if Rafe goes to prison for aiding and abetting a murderer?"

It's the first time anyone's said it out loud. *Murderer.* Cole was murdered. Someone killed him on purpose. His death wasn't a terrible twist of fate, one of those freak accidents that occur on the water, reminding us how small we are in the face of the ocean. I glance at Gabriel. His face is twisted up as though he can hardly breathe.

"We won't let Rafe—or Darren—get away with it," I promise. I put my hand on Gabriel's back. I look to Pope for reassurance. "Right?"

"Right," Pope agrees. "You can't argue with forensic evidence. It'll prove what happened to him."

Somehow, Pope's promise doesn't actually reassure me. Sure, the evidence will prove what happened to him.

But it won't tell us who did it.

CHAPTER 22

POPE

JOHN B DRIVES ME TO WORK IN THE MORNING SO THAT I CAN bring the surfboard with me. I'll log it in as evidence, but first I want to show it to Dr. A—proof that if Cole was strangled, it wasn't his own leash that did him in. Someone could've used a piece of the same sort of material—you can buy an extra leash at any surf shop—in an attempt to make it look like a terrible accident.

John B is quiet on the drive over, and I guess I can't blame him. It's not like what happened to Cole has anything to do with what happened to Big John, except that it kind of does, because they both went missing on the water. Cole's body was found, but it could have easily been lost. Our government puts so much time and resources into exploring the space above us—when I was a little kid, I fantasized about life on other planets, taking a trip to the moon, colonizing Mars—but there's just as much to explore in our planet's oceans. There are life-forms we've never glimpsed—plants and fish and sea creatures we don't have names for, every bit as alien as the little green men that might come from the sky. Beneath the water's surface are thousands of years' worth of missing ships, bodies, treasures. Items that will never be found, no matter how hard we look.

Normally, quiet doesn't bother me. It gives me time to think about things, like the secrets hiding deep in our oceans. But this morning, I'm thinking about how close Kie and Gabriel were sitting in John B's backyard last night. How she rubbed her hand up and down his back when he was distraught over what had happened to his best friend. It's a terrible thing to be jealous of—she was touching him because he was grief-stricken—but it still makes me itchy, thinking about the way she touched him. I glance at John B. Did he notice, too? Or would he think I'm being petty, feeling envy at a time like this?

Even if it's petty, I bet John B's noticed the way Kie looks at Gabriel. Like she'd drop everything to go around the world chasing waves with him. We just got Kie back from the Kook school. We can't lose her to Gabriel now.

"Door-to-door service," John B says as he pulls up to the police station.

"Thanks for the ride."

John B shrugs. "Anytime."

He says it like it's no big deal—of course he'll always drive me wherever I need to go, because I'm a Pogue and that's what Pogues do, without question.

I haul Cole's board out of the back of the van and head down into the morgue.

"Dr. A!" I shout. "Wait till you see what I've got!"

I expect to see Cole's body where I left it, but the mortuary table is empty. Dr. Anderson is in her office with the door closed. She's typing something into her computer, her glasses slipping down over the bridge of her nose, her hair neatly pulled back into a ponytail. I prop Cole's surfboard against the glass wall of her office and knock on the door.

"Dr. Anderson?"

"Come in."

"Where's Cole?" I ask.

"In the cabinet," she answers. Mortuary cabinets are the low-temperature refrigerated compartments that are used to keep dead bodies cool and preserved. They line the walls of the morgue.

"Do you want me to prep him?" I begin to turn without waiting for an answer, but the doctor stops me.

"No need," Dr. Anderson says. "I completed the autopsy this morning."

"Without me?"

Dr. Anderson raises an eyebrow. "You may find this hard to believe, Pope, but I managed to conduct quite a few exams before you became my intern."

"I didn't mean it like that—" I begin, but the doctor cuts me off.

"I know you were looking forward to solving a mystery, but this job isn't fun and games."

"I didn't mean it like that—" I repeat, but she cuts me off again.

"I certainly hope not. I have to admit, Pope, at first I found your attitude impressive, but I've begun to worry that your enthusiasm means that you're not taking this job seriously."

"I take this job very seriously," I scramble. I thought Dr. Anderson liked how eager I was.

"Autopsies aren't *fun*, Pope. You didn't miss out on an adventure because you didn't get to examine the dead body of a teenage boy. This is serious work, the only way to give a grieving family closure so they can move on with their lives after a terrible loss."

"I know that," I say quietly, thinking of Gabriel.

"I certainly hope you do." Dr. Anderson adjusts her glasses.

"I hope you don't mind my asking," I begin carefully, "but what was it?"

"What was what?" Dr. Anderson snaps impatiently.

"Cole's official cause of death."

Dr. Anderson looks as though she's never heard such a stupid question. "Drowning."

"Drowning?" I echo. "What about the leash marks around his neck?"

"Upon closer examination, it was clear that they weren't rope—" Dr. A waves her hand. "Sorry, leash marks at all but scratches, probably from the fight that Cole reportedly got into before the competition. We have multiple witnesses confirming a scuffle at The Wreck three days before he went missing." She pauses meaningfully, and I wonder if she knows that I am one of those multiple witnesses. She continues: "Cole must have fallen from his board, hit his head—either on the board or on another object beneath the water—lost consciousness, and drowned."

"No way," I say before I can stop myself.

"Are you questioning my opinion?" Dr. Anderson asks sharply. "Or have you forgotten which one of us is the doctor here?"

"It's not that, it's just—I was there that night, when Darren and Cole got into it at The Wreck. Darren threw a punch, but he didn't scratch Cole. And I looked at Cole's body yesterday—there was no indication that he hit his head."

Dr. Anderson narrows her eyes. "When?"

"When what?"

"When did you have time to so thoroughly examine the deceased's body?"

Crap. I was supposed to cover Cole up after Dr. Anderson left. I definitely wasn't supposed to examine him unsupervised.

"Do you realize the sort of trouble you could get into? The sort of trouble you could get *me* into? You are not authorized to handle our patients without my express supervision, to say nothing of your gross disrespect for the dead."

"I wasn't being disrespectful!" I think about the care I took tracing Cole's body. "I was trying to help!"

"There's nothing helpful about breaking the rules," Dr. Anderson counters. She gets up from behind her desk and walks into the main room of the morgue. "What's this?" she asks when she sees the surfboard propped against the glass.

"Cole's surfboard," I answer quickly. "My friends found it yesterday. As you can see, the leash is still attached, which indicates that Cole must have been strangled by something else."

"I already told you, Cole wasn't strangled at all. He drowned."

"But the marks—"

"Pope, it turned out they aren't marks at all. Sometimes a scratch is just a scratch. It only upsets the deceased's loved ones to make something out of nothing. It's harder for the bereaved to accept their loss if they think their loved one's death is a mystery to be solved."

"But what about—"

"In fact, the intact leash only proves how much more likely it is that Cole fell from his board, got hit on the head, lost consciousness, and drowned."

"Then why wasn't he found with his board? Wouldn't his ankle still have been strapped to his leash?"

Dr. Anderson shakes her head. "Not if he'd forgotten to fasten it. Think about it, Pope. Which explanation makes more sense: that Cole drowned in the ocean because he was irresponsibly engaged in a dangerous sport, or that he was strangled by a phantom surfboard leash?"

I have to admit, Dr. Anderson has a point.

"Speaking of breaking the rules," Dr. Anderson continues, "you brought that board down here when it should have been logged in to evidence upstairs."

"I'll bring it up right away!" I promise. I never thought of myself as a rule-breaker. At least, not in the context of this internship. But it turns out I've broken quite a few rules in the past twenty-four hours.

"Good. And why don't you take the rest of the day off?"

"Take the day off?" I echo. I just got here. I feel like I'm being punished.

"I understand that you knew Cole—maybe this case is a little bit too personal for you. And you've shown that I can't trust you to behave appropriately when you're clouded by your emotions."

Just a few days ago, I felt like Dr. Anderson had already taught me all I needed to know; now she looks so disappointed in me that my cheeks grow hot. I feel the glowing letter of recommendation she'd promised to write for my college applications slipping away.

"In fact," she continues, "Cole's body's being cremated in the morning, and his remains will be sent home to his family in California. I think you should stay away until he's gone."

"I don't need to—"

"Pope, this isn't a request."

I nod heavily. I bring the surfboard upstairs and submit it to the police, telling them exactly where John B said they found it, but then I realize that none of the details matter, now that Dr. Anderson's determined the cause of death and ruled it an accident. They probably won't even examine the board. They'll ship it home to Cole's parents along with his ashes like it's an extension of his body. I don't spook easy, but the thought makes me shiver.

I walk home slowly. Dad will wonder why I'm home early, and I don't want to tell him that my boss practically kicked me out.

Was I really trying to invent a mystery, like Dr. Anderson said? Am I too close to this case? I didn't know Cole well, but he reminded me of JJ, and maybe that's enough to make the loss feel personal.

But she praised me for finding the leash marks yesterday, I'm sure of that. I was so proud.

But Dr. A is brilliant at her job. She's been a generous mentor all summer long. She knows what she's talking about. She must have taken a closer look this morning and realized I'd blown the "evidence" way out of proportion. She must've seen a bump on his head that I'm too inexperienced to notice. I'll apologize once I'm back in the morgue. I can't screw up this internship. I need that letter of recommendation.

I pull my phone from my pocket and text Kie.

Can you and Gabriel meet me at Heyward's?

I feel terrible for misleading Gabriel. Cole's death isn't a mystery to be solved but a tragedy to be mourned.

Gabriel deserves to know the truth.

CHAPTER 23

POPE

GABRIEL KICKS AT THE DUMPSTER BEHIND THE STORE. OR HE starts by kicking it, anyway. His kicking turns into punching. Kie reaches for him, but I pull her back.

"He'll hurt you!"

"He wouldn't hurt me," Kie insists, but she stops struggling against my hold. Gabriel might not intend to hurt her, but I'm pretty sure that right now, at this moment, he'd hurt just about anything that came between him and Pop's dumpster.

I told him what Dr. Anderson said. Cole drowned. No foul play, no further explanation to make what happened make sense. Just an accident, a twist of fate. The sort of story parents will tell their kids when they're trying to talk them out of surfing, keep them from heading into the water alone, when there's no lifeguard on duty. A cautionary tale.

I don't know much about Cole, but from what I've heard, I think he'd hate that.

"What's going on out here?!" Pop comes through the back exit shouting.

When he sees Gabriel, though, he quiets. He doesn't try to stop him. He lets Gabriel wear himself out, and when Gabriel finally relents, chest heaving and knuckles bloody, Pop doesn't yell at him for the mess he's made of the dumpster. He doesn't even scold me for coming around with my good-for-nothing friends and making a racket behind the store.

Instead he says, "Come inside, son. We'll get you cleaned up." Pop walks back inside slowly, his baggy cargo shorts and oversized t-shirt hanging loosely on his body.

Inside the store, Pop grabs the first aid kit from one of the shelves behind the counter, taking out some antiseptic spray and bandages. He cleans and wraps Gabriel's hands wordlessly, carefully, like there's nothing the least bit unusual about what's happening, like he's done this a thousand times before.

Finally, Gabriel says, "I'm sorry about your dumpster."

"No apology necessary. Old metal trash heap had it coming." Pop smiles just a little, and Gabriel smiles back.

Scientific Question: What the hell has gotten into Pop?

Hypothesis: When Pop sees someone grieving, does he actually know exactly the right things to do and say?

"Son," Pop begins, and it's the second time he's called Gabriel "son," "I don't know if this will help, but for what it's worth, I know how you feel."

165

Gabriel doesn't argue. Instead he nods. "Because of Howie Rivers?"

Pop nods solemnly. "Yeah. Because of Howie Rivers."

"Who's Howie Rivers?" I ask.

Pop turns to Kie and me like he forgot we were here. I can practically see him decide that there's no point in keeping the story from us. If he doesn't tell us, Gabriel will.

"Howie was my partner."

"What do you mean, partner?" Kie asks. "Business partner? Did he run the store with you?"

Pop shakes his head. "Howie and I towed in together."

"You tow-in surfed, Dad?" I ask, filled with shock.

"Wow!" Kie adds.

Pop laughs. "I wasn't always this old, you know. There was a time when I was just as young and fit as the two of you." He looks wistful, and I don't think I've ever seen my dad look wistful. He goes on: "Howie was the best surfer I knew. We were tow-in surfing in the early days, when it was all experimentation and instinct. There were no rules, no competitions. Just a few of us trying to get to the biggest waves we could find."

Gabriel looks incredulous. "You didn't know that your dad was one of the pioneers of the sport?"

I shake my head. Pop never told me, and it's not like it ever occurred to me to google my own parents.

"Howie was the better surfer, so I usually drove the Jet Ski. And then one day at Mavericks—"

"Mavericks?" I interrupt.

"It's a surf break off the coast of Northern California," Kie explains.

"It has a name?"

"Lots of them do. Jaws in Hawaii, Teahupo'o in the South Pacific, Nazaré in Portugal . . ."

Pop continues: "I felt Howie let go of the rope, and when I turned back to watch him—I used to say I had the best view, watching him from the water like that—he wasn't there. I mean, he'd *vanished*. No sign of him. No board, no shorts, no leash—nothing."

"Did they ever find his body?" Kie asks. Pop shakes his head.

"I drove around on the ski for hours, till it ran out of juice and I had to swim back to shore. A bunch of us searched for a few days after that. The Coast Guard got involved. But eventually, they called off the hunt. The ocean's swallowed thousands of us over the years. Couldn't expect her to give Howie back just because he's my friend." Pop's Adam's apple bounces up and down as he swallows. "It took me years to accept that he was really gone. It was like some part of me thought he'd turn up one day and razz me for the mistake I'd made."

"What mistake?" I ask.

"I don't know, Pope. I thought I must've done something wrong. Why else would my best friend, the best surfer I know, have died?" He looks at Gabriel meaningfully.

We sit in silence for a few minutes. I try to put the pieces together in my head, but it's impossible to connect the father I know to the story he's telling. They're like pieces from two entirely different puzzles.

But it does explain why the professional surfers have been hanging out around the store the last few days. And maybe it also explains Alan Thomas and the cold shoulder Pop gave him when he came in for some Advil—I'd looked him up the day after the fight at The Wreck and seen that he used to surf before he went over to the manager side. He and Pop are around the same age.

"Is that how you know Alan?" I ask.

Pop nods. "Alan was a surfer from a few towns over, just kind of came on the scene out of nowhere. I never had much to do with him until he cheated in one of our competitions and I got blamed for it." Pop's voice turns bitter, suggesting he never quite got over being scapegoated, which I can definitely understand.

"Was he any good?"

"Not like Howie. Not even like me. He was the sort who relied on tricks like dropping in on another surfer's wave to throw competitors off their game. And he still never won a contest." Pop smiles grimly. "He was there, that day at Mavericks, on the wave just behind Howie and me. He always said he never saw what happened, but—"

"You think he dropped in on Howie?" Gabriel interjects.

"I don't know. I really don't. Like I said, sometimes there's no explanation. Even if he'd dropped in, a million other tiny little links in the chain had to line up for that to be the day that Howie disappeared. Sometimes the ocean takes over and surfers—even the most skilled surfers—drown. It's no one's and everyone's fault all at once."

"I know you're right," Gabriel says, "but I can't help thinking, if I'd gone out there with Cole that morning . . ."

"And if I'd towed Howie onto that wave thirty seconds sooner or later. If I'd beat him up the day before so that he'd been too injured to surf at all. If I'd broken my leg so I couldn't tow him in. If only it had rained that day. If Mavericks hadn't broken that year—you see what I'm saying, son? All those ifs are gonna kill you. Don't waste years of your life like I did."

I know Pop isn't telling this story for my benefit. In fact, if Gabriel hadn't battled our dumpster, maybe Pop would've gone the rest of his life without telling me any of this. But I have about a million questions. I feel surprised knowing more about Pop, but also sad that I didn't know any of this before. Often it's like Pop is this robotic workaholic who does the same thing every single day. I haven't known anything different of him. All of this is a lot to process, but I think it's helped me to know my dad better. For that, I guess, I'm grateful.

"Did you ever surf again after that?" I ask, wondering, my brain popping with thoughts and questions. "Do you ever wish you still did?"

169

Pop takes a deep breath. "I think that's enough for today." He nods at Gabriel. This time, when Kie moves to him, I don't try to stop her. She wraps her arms around him and he collapses, sobbing.

Pop's right. Now's not the time for me to pepper him with questions, however many I have. He told his story to comfort Gabriel, and now it's time for Kie and me to take over.

But before Pop walks away, I shoot him a look, letting him know that when the time is right, I'm going to ask him to tell me everything.

CHAPTER 24

KIE

"NO WAY." JJ SHAKES HIS HEAD. "I DON'T BELIEVE IT."

"It's the truth," Pope insists. He looks apologetic. "I never should've told you anything before Dr. Anderson completed her exam."

"It's okay," Gabriel assures him. "You were trying to help."

Pope nods, but he still looks guilty.

"At least we know what happened now," Pope says finally. "I hope that gives you some sense of, I don't know . . . closure. Peace."

Gabriel nods, though the look on his face tells me that peaceful is about the last thing he feels. Still, he doesn't want Pope to feel bad. If anyone should feel bad, it's me. I'm the one who guilted Pope into sharing whatever he learned about Cole's death before it was official. He knew better, but he did it because I asked him to.

"Am I the only one making any sense here?" JJ practically shouts. The rest of us turn to him in surprise. JJ is a lot of things, but he's definitely not the most sensible Pogue.

We're back at the Chateau. I'm not at work (again), Pope was sent home early, Gabriel's still in town, and John B and JJ are hanging out.

"Do any of you really believe that Pope would've missed something as obvious as a bump on the head?" JJ asks.

"Dr. Anderson said—"

"Screw Dr. Anderson. I know you, like, worship her or whatever, but that doesn't mean she can't make a mistake."

"I don't worship her," Pope insists. "But she's a gifted doctor—"

"And you're a gifted intern," JJ interjects. "Tell me the truth, Pope. Do you really, really believe you could have missed something that significant when you examined the body?"

Pope closes his eyes. We sit there in silence staring at him for so long that if it weren't for the way he's holding himself—straight, like an arrow, his eyes screwed shut like he's thinking extra hard—I would think he fell asleep.

"I don't know," Pope answers finally, opening his eyes.

"See?" JJ shouts, like that proves everything when, in fact, it doesn't prove anything. It leaves us with even more questions than when we started.

"What should we do?" John B asks finally. "Gabriel, this is your call—Cole was your best friend."

Gabriel's sitting next to me, so close I can feel the warmth from his body. His back curls into a C as he slumps in his seat.

"I know what to do!" JJ says with a definitive nod. "We need to talk to Rafe."

"Rafe?" I echo.

"It's like we said the other day. He's supposedly the last person to see Cole alive. Maybe he saw more than he let on. Maybe he saw Cole lose his balance, hit his head. Then at least we'd know that the autopsy report is accurate."

"It's not a bad idea," John B says.

"Rafe's not going to tell us when he wouldn't tell the police," I point out reasonably.

"The police don't have our powers of persuasion," JJ answers with a grin.

✳ ✳ ✳

HOURS LATER, JOHN B PULLS UP IN FRONT OF A ROW OF MANsions sitting behind tall privets, long snake-shaped driveways, and iron gates.

"Not here," JJ whispers. "Park down the street."

"How're we gonna see Rafe leave from down the block?" John B points out reasonably.

"Yeah, but if we stay here, someone will recognize the van," I say.

"C'mon, JJ, this was your brilliant plan," John B says.

"No. My plan was to grab Rafe, force him into the van, scare him into talking. I never said anything about *how*."

"So you thought you'd leave it up to us to work out the logistics?" Pope asks.

"Logistics are your specialty, Pope."

Pope can't argue with that.

"Okay, so what do we do?" Pope asks. "This party could go all night. We can't sit parked here for hours, waiting for Rafe to come out."

"If he comes out at all," John B adds. "You know Rafe—he's as likely to pass out on someone's sofa as to head home at the end of the night."

"Listen, guys," Gabriel chimes in, "I appreciate all you're doing for me, but maybe this isn't a good idea. I mean, if it's this hard to ask the guy a simple question, maybe . . ."

He trails off like he doesn't have the energy to finish the thought. I think about the guy I met on the beach just last week: his easy grin, his boundless energy, the way he rode the waves and smiled at his friend's skills on the water. He looks . . . paler, somehow. And not the kind of pale you get because you missed a couple days out on the ocean. I mean he looks somehow less substantial. Like he's lost.

"No," I say firmly. "We're staying. John B, you pull the van down the street like JJ said."

"Okay, then how're we going to get Rafe?"

"*We're* not going to get him," I correct. "*I* am."

I know these kids. I went to school with them last year. They're probably drunk enough that they don't even remember I don't attend Kook Academy anymore.

I've even been inside this house before, for a party last fall. Ryan Bradley's an only child and his parents are out of town a lot. When JJ said he'd heard about a Kook party tonight, I bet it was here.

I pull my hair into a top knot and adjust my tank top and shorts so it looks less like I dressed for hanging out doing nothing all day and more like I'm trying to be sexy for a party. I dig around in the van until I find an old tube of lip gloss. I use it to brighten my lips, my eyelids, my cheeks. It's not much, but I can tell it's noticeable from the way the guys stare at me as I get out of the van. Even Gabriel's looking.

I'm glad my back is to him so he can't see the way his gaze makes me smile.

I walk right through the front door. I feel like at any moment someone's going to sound the alarm, set the dogs on me, but all my presence earns is a few nods and "heys" from my former classmates.

Ryan's house is one of those southern-style mansions with pillars on the front porch like his mom imagines herself as being Scarlett O'Hara from *Gone with the Wind* (gross on so many levels). No joke, they have an Irish setter named Scarlett (also gross, naming your dog after one of the most famous fictional enslavers). Inside, the foyer has gleaming white marble floors, though I notice black scuff marks from where someone tracked in dirt. In front of me is a staircase wide enough for six people to stand side by side, the banister carved from honey-colored wood and each step covered in thick champagne-tinted carpet.

This party is identical to the one I went to last fall. The foyer is littered with the same Kook princesses wearing high heels and short dresses, the same Kook princes who went overboard on cologne before they left the house, all holding the same red plastic cups overflowing with cheap beer, spilling and staining the floor. It's all I can do to keep from gagging. The house's sound system—surely installed by his parents to play classical music at dinner parties—is turned up as loud as it can go, so it feels like the band is shouting rather than singing.

The fact that this party is exactly the same as the one I went to months ago means that I know exactly where to find Rafe. Rafe doesn't go for plastic cups and cheap beer. He'll be upstairs, in Ryan's dad's study. Last fall, Ryan called it the "inner sanctum" and invited Sarah and me there. She and I held hands as we walked up the stairs, laughing. I can't believe I was ever excited to be invited to join the popular kids. For a few months, that was so important to me that I missed surf practice, trading dreams of chasing waves around the world for top-shelf liquor and fancy dresses, just like my parents wanted me to.

I'm so lost in my memories that I don't notice that Sarah's standing right in front of me until she says, "What the hell are you doing here?"

So much for hoping that everyone might have forgotten I don't go to school with them anymore. Sarah's blond hair is loose around her shoulders. She's wearing a yellow sundress with wedge heels, and her eyes are ringed with thick black eyeliner. She's wearing a gold necklace with a single diamond charm that I know her dad gave her for her last birthday.

"Ryan invited me," I say. It's not entirely a lie. Back in the fall, he said I was welcome any time. He says that to literally every girl at school.

Sarah doesn't question my invitation, but she seems skeptical that I'd accept it. "Thought you never wanted to be caught on the Kook side of town again."

"I'm not caught," I counter. "I wanted to come."

Sarah shakes her head in disbelief.

"Shouldn't you be cheering Topper on while he, I don't know, plays pool or video games or whatever it is he's into now?"

It always stuns me, how content Sarah is to sit around doing nothing while Topper actually participates, like she's part of the scenery. For a while there, she convinced me it was *fun*, her boyfriend doing actual activities as we watched. Video games aren't meant to be spectator sports.

"Or while he wins a surf competition," Sarah replies hotly, her eyes narrowed.

"Actually, Topper came in second. Second place is first loser." I can't believe I'm saying that. I don't believe it. Second place is a big deal.

Sarah's eyes flash with something I don't quite recognize. Instead of contempt, it looks like concern.

"I saw you wipe out the other day . . ." she begins.

No way. I'm not falling for her false sympathy.

"At least I was actually on the water instead of standing on the sidelines," I scoff, then shove my way past her and up the stairs.

CHAPTER 25

KIE

RYAN'S DAD'S STUDY LOOKS EXACTLY LIKE I REMEMBER IT: the plush burgundy carpet, the dark wood-paneled walls, the shelves covered with books whose spines have never been broken.

Ryan's in here with a couple of guys I recognize as his crew from school, and luckily Rafe is one of them. The boys are all wearing practically the same thing: light khaki pants or shorts, topped with buttondowns in various shades of blue with the sleeves rolled up. Fortunately—or, really, unfortunately—no one stops me from walking in. For guys like this—straight, heteronormative, steeped in toxic masculinity—girls are merely decoration, and the more of them dotting the landscape, the better. Like Sarah, most of the girls in here are wearing sundresses and high heels. In the guys' minds, they're probably interchangeable with one another. I have to swallow to keep my disgust from exploding up my throat and out my mouth. If anyone ever needed a lecture on women's rights, it's these guys.

But at least tonight, I'm turning the power dynamic around, using the fact that they see me as an object, as pleasing to the eye as wall sconces and chandeliers, against them. I'm using it to get what I want.

And what I want is for Rafe to leave with me.

Just the thought—*I want Rafe to leave with me*—is enough to make me gag, but I picture Gabriel waiting in the van, desperate to understand what happened to his best friend. I think of what I would do if something happened to JJ or Pope or John B, the lengths I would go to in order to understand their injuries, disappearance, or death. I think about Big John and all the questions John B has never gotten answers to.

I can do this.

I see Rafe and walk over to him. I can already smell the alcohol on him, like a strong odor, which tells me he's been drinking for a while. It's not unusual for Rafe; I've known him long enough to know that this is how he forgets he's Ward's son. Rafe's blond hair is the exact same shade as Sarah's. He's wearing khaki shorts that go to his knees, and his blue button-down shirt is striped like seersucker.

"Hi, Rafe," I say.

"Hi . . . Kie," Rafe says (well, slurs).

I sit on the shiny leather couch beside Rafe and ask if I can have a sip of his drink. He hands me a crystal tumbler etched with diamond shapes. I take a sip of the brown liquid, recognizing the flavor of good Kentucky bourbon, but I act like I've never had something so strong before.

Rafe laughs as I pretend to have trouble swallowing. "We can get you something more your speed, little girl," he promises. Then he literally snaps at a girl sitting on the other side of the coffee table to pass me her drink instead. Her diamond-etched glass is full of something in a shade of pink I'm pretty sure doesn't exist in nature.

I sip her drink and smile like it's the yummiest thing I've ever had, even though it tastes like cough syrup and I'd rather have bourbon.

Rafe and the other guys are playing poker, chips and cards spread out on the table in front of us. None of the girls are actually playing. Instead, they act like watching a bunch of guys playing poker is as riveting as sitting in a movie theater for the latest Marvel movie.

I sip my sticky drink and lean into Rafe, sneaking a peek at his hand. He has two pair.

"Fold," I whisper.

"Why?"

I nod at Ryan across the table. "Ryan's got something big."

"How can you tell?"

"See the way he's tapping his thigh?"

Rafe nods.

"He did that in algebra last semester when he cheated on his test. He knew he was going to get an A no matter what."

Rafe looks at me like he's seeing me for the first time. I can feel his gaze taking in my tank top and short shorts.

"Whatever the lady says," he promises, placing his cards facedown on the table. When Ryan reveals a full house, Rafe gives me a high five.

"Looks like I found my lucky charm," he says. "Kiara Carrera, the half-Kook wonder."

I pretend being called half Kook doesn't offend me. That's how Rafe and his friends thought of me for the year I went to school with them: not entirely a Pogue or a Kook. No matter how well I fit in—the right outfits, the right parties, the right friends—it was a constant reminder that I'd always be an outsider. For a few weeks, maybe even a month, I hated that feeling. But after a while, I was glad to know I would never fit in. The last thing I wanted to be was a Kook.

I advise Rafe for a couple more hands. But on the fourth hand, when he has three of a kind, I tell Rafe, "Go all in."

He grins at me. "Whatever my lucky charm says." I have to keep myself from shuddering when he refers to me as *his* anything. Rafe pushes all his chips into the center of the table. Ryan calls. Rafe doesn't notice that Ryan's tapping his thigh again.

Ryan reveals his cards: a straight.

"Crap!" Rafe shouts, throwing his cards down. He turns to me angrily. "Why'd you tell me to go all in?"

I swallow the urge to point out that he has no right to be angry at me. I was just giving him advice; I'm not actually a magic lucky charm. But instead I say, "Look on the bright side."

"What bright side?" Rafe pouts.

"Now we can get out of here."

Rafe's scowl twists into a smile as he catches my meaning. He grabs my hand and pulls me up to stand, like I'm a prize instead of an actual person.

"Later, losers," he calls to Ryan and his friends.

In the hallway, Rafe says, "This place has got, like, a dozen bedrooms," and tugs me down the hall.

"No way." I shake my head. "I'm not hooking up where anyone could walk in. Your sister's around. You know what she'll say if she sees us together?" I make a face like I'm horrified.

"I don't care what she says."

I drop my voice an octave. "Let's not risk it." I release my hair from its bun, feeling it fall across my shoulders. "I've got a better idea. Come on."

I lead Rafe down the stairs and out the front door, rolling my eyes as soon as my back is turned. Boys like him are so easy. I pull my phone from my pocket. "Just texting my parents that I'm staying with a friend tonight." Rafe is too pleased to question it. Instead, I text the guys.

We're heading out the door. Be ready.

We walk down the long driveway and through the gate. I turn us in the direction of the van.

"Where are we going, gorgeous?" Rafe asks. He holds my hand, his fingers playing on my inner wrist in a way I'm sure he thinks is sexy and suggestive.

"You'll see," I promise, and Rafe grins, his teeth white in the moonlight, just as John B pops out from under the hedges.

"Boy will you see," John B promises. I duck to the side as he lunges for Rafe, who looks entirely dumbfounded by this turn of events.

JJ stuffs a rag into Rafe's mouth to keep him from shouting.

"Where'd you find that?" I ask.

"The floor of the Twinkie," JJ answers, which is almost enough to make me feel sorry for Rafe. I don't think John B has ever actually cleaned the van. There's no telling what kind of trash is inside.

"Kie's covered in Kook cooties!" JJ whisper-shouts as he, John B, and Pope drag Rafe around the corner and toward the van's open back door.

"Ugh, don't remind me," I say with a shudder. "Where's Gabriel?"

"Getaway driver," JJ whispers. Rafe is struggling with all his might, but the guys have barely broken a sweat. It's not really a fair fight, three against one.

"I'm surprised you got him to agree to that."

"Pope insisted," John B explains. "Said this was a Pogue thing."

"Figured there was no reason for him to risk getting into trouble," Pope explains. "What if one of Rafe's friends saw us?"

I smile at Pope, thankful that he was looking out for Gabriel.

"He wasn't happy about it," JJ says. "Kept arguing that we were only doing this because of him."

"How'd you convince him to cooperate?"

"We're not here because of Gabriel," JJ answers flatly. "We're here because of Cole."

Even though JJ knew Cole for only a couple days, it's clear he felt a kinship with him. I imagine what might have happened if Cole hadn't died. Maybe he and JJ would've become fast friends. Maybe JJ would've been the one taking off to chase waves around the world, not me.

No, JJ would never leave the OBX like that.

He and John B heave Rafe's squirming, squirrelly body into the van and slam the door shut behind them. JJ holds Rafe's wrists so he can't pull the rag out of his mouth and start screaming. Gabriel's waiting in the driver's seat, just like the guys said.

"By the way," I say, unable to keep my feminist rant inside anymore, "if you ever find yourself at a party where the girls are treated like wallpaper, promise me you will turn tail and run in the other direction."

"What if we stay at the party but treat the girls like actual human beings instead of wallpaper?" John B suggests.

"Even better," I agree. "And also? Don't be so stupid as to leave a party with a girl who's inexplicably interested in you after never having given you the time of day."

Rafe's eyes grow wide as it dawns on him that my flirting was all an act.

"Ugh, I feel like I need to take a shower." I shudder.

"Plenty of time for that later," JJ promises.

"Okay, we got him," John B says. "Now what?"

"Let's get out of here," I say.

Gabriel puts the van into gear and drives.

CHAPTER 26

POPE

JJ'S COME UP WITH A LOT OF RIDICULOUS SCHEMES OVER THE years, but I think this may be my least favorite of his harebrained plans. None of his other plans have involved kidnapping a Kook—albeit temporarily and when said Kook is so drunk he probably won't remember this in the morning.

But it's not like I can protest when it's my fault we're here on Figure 8 in the first place. I'm the one who told Gabriel about the leash marks on Cole's neck. I'm the reason Gabriel doesn't believe his best friend drowned.

So, here I am, sitting in the back of the van while John B drives us to the Evergreen Bayou to question Rafe. That was JJ's idea, too: to jog Rafe's memory by taking him back to the scene of the crime.

"We don't know there was a crime," I protested. "And we definitely don't know that Rafe had anything to do with it."

"Relax, Pope, it's just an expression," JJ insisted, but I didn't think so. It stopped being "just an expression" after a lifeless body was found nearby.

Scientific Question: What do four Pogues + one out-of-town surfer + one Kook in the van add up to?

Conclusion: Results pending further investigation.

John B drives onto the sand—at some point, he and Gabriel switched places—then puts the Twinkie into park.

"Let's get this show on the road," he says. JJ grins. The two of them wrestle Rafe out of the back of the van, his blond hair flopping above his forehead in a way that, in another context, he'd probably think was charming. Personally, I think the guy needs a haircut.

Gabriel, Kie, and I follow the guys out of the back of the van. John B and JJ sit Rafe up on his knees, his bare skin against the sand. I notice that Rafe lost one of his shoes.

"Kie, did Rafe have both of his shoes when you two left Ryan's house?" I ask.

"Huh?"

"Did he have his shoes on? Because if not, then he lost his shoe on the street outside the van, and some other Kook will find it and they might figure out—"

Kie shakes her head, her curls bouncing in the wind off the ocean. "No one will think anything of it. They all saw how drunk Rafe was when he left the party."

John B crouches in front of Rafe and removes the rag from his mouth. JJ stands behind him, holding one of his arms. He motions for me to stand behind Rafe and take his other arm.

I do it, but I don't hold on nearly as tight as JJ does. There are five of us and one of him.

"What the hell?" Rafe shouts. "Help! Help!" he calls out. "I've been kidnapped by a bunch of good-for-nothing Pogue losers!"

"Aw, c'mon, Rafe," JJ says, tugging on Rafe's arm. "No need for name-calling."

"We just want to ask you a few questions," John B adds, keeping his voice calm. Somewhere along the way, he and JJ decided to play good cop, bad cop.

"Why the hell should I answer your questions?" Rafe spits out.

"Because if you don't we're going to beat the shit out of you," JJ says, then laughs. I honestly can't tell if he's just trying to scare Rafe into cooperating or if he actually plans on hurting Rafe.

"No one has to get hurt." John B holds up his hands like he's here to keep the peace. "We just want to know what you saw the morning Cole went missing."

"I already told the police—"

"We know you did," John B says, his voice still calm. "Now we want you to tell us."

"Tell you what?" Rafe says. "I told them—I came here to surf just for fun, and Cole was here, too."

"Was anyone else here?" Gabriel jumps in. "Was Darren here?"

Rafe blinks. "Darren?" he echoes. "No, no one else was in the water but Cole and me. By the time I left them, Cole was still on the water. He looked fine."

John B shoots me a look over the top of Rafe's head and I nod.

Yeah, I answer silently. *I heard it, too.*

"What do you mean *them*?" John B asks.

"Huh?"

"You said by the time you left *them* on the beach."

"I meant—I meant by the time I left him on the beach."

"Then why'd you say *them*, moron?" JJ asks, tugging on Rafe's arm so he winces.

Rafe lifts his head up, looking first at John B, then at Kie and Gabriel standing just behind him. He cranes his neck to see JJ and me over his shoulders.

"I know you're not very good at math, Rafe," JJ says, "but there are five of us and one of you. I think you should answer John B's question."

At once, Rafe pulls his arm out of my grip and swings, throwing a punch at John B, who dances out of the way, but not before Rafe clips his nose.

"Crap!" John B shouts, holding his hand to the bridge of his nose. JJ's grip on Rafe's other arm is so tight that Rafe can't get free, but he pulls JJ down on top of him.

"Let me see," Kie says, reaching for John B's face, just as Gabriel dives to the ground to help JJ regain control over Rafe.

"Pope!" JJ shouts, and I realize that I'm just standing here watching. I reach for Rafe's other arm, but he swings wildly. He's too drunk to hit very hard, though he manages to scratch my neck. Something about the sensation reminds me why we're here.

Because Cole died.

Because he had red marks on his neck that Dr. Anderson called scratches.

I grab Rafe's arm and twist it behind his back, pulling him back onto his knees. Rafe comes up spitting sand out of his mouth, shaking it out of his hair.

"Answer the question, Cameron," I say, my voice low and even. "Who else was there that morning?"

"Fine," Rafe spits out. "I wanted another chance to show Alan my skills."

Kie scoffs at Rafe's use of the word *skills* just as Gabriel asks angrily, "How'd that work out? Is Alan your manager now, too?"

Rafe sniffs angrily. "No. Slimy piece of crap thinks he's too good for me."

"Or he thinks you're not good enough for him," JJ counters.

"That's the same thing, JJ," Kie points out.

"It's not the same thing!" JJ insists.

"Why didn't you tell the police that Alan was here?" I ask.

"How do you know what I told the police?"

"We know everything, rich boy," JJ supplies. "Now answer my friend's question. Why didn't you tell the police that Alan was here that morning?"

"None of your business."

JJ tugs on Rafe's arm and Rafe howls. JJ laughs and says, "I can do this all night and all day."

"Fine!" Rafe shouts. "I didn't tell them because of what Alan said to me."

"What did Alan say?" Gabriel asks, his eyes wide and alert.

"He . . ." Rafe pauses, like whatever this is, it's difficult to say, it's a terrible secret he thinks we won't believe. "I met up with Alan that morning at Evergreen Bayou to try and . . . offer him money to take me on as a client. But he laughed in my face. He said . . . he said I wasn't a good enough surfer to go pro."

JJ starts laughing so hard he almost drops Rafe's arm.

"Well, shit, man, I could've told you that," he says, out of breath with laughter. "Any of us could've told you that. Even Pope could've told you that."

"Hey!" I protest.

"No offense, man," JJ explains. "Just that you're not as into surfing as the rest of us."

Rafe continues, his breathing slowing. "He said there wasn't enough money in the world for him to represent me. I didn't want my dad to know that I couldn't close the deal with Alan."

Suddenly, Rafe's arm goes limp beneath my grip.

"He passed out," Kie says, unable to hide her disgust.

"Let's get out of here," JJ says, dropping Rafe's arm and heading for the van.

"Not without him," John B says.

"Why?"

"Because if he wakes up here, he might wonder how he got here. But if he wakes up at home, he'll figure he stumbled home drunk and passed out. No way will he remember this tomorrow."

"And even if he does," Kie adds, "he'll be too embarrassed to tell anyone. No Kook wants to admit that he got outwitted by a bunch of Pogues."

"Plus me." Gabriel holds up his hand like we're in a classroom.

Kie turns to Gabriel and grins. "For tonight, you can be an honorary Pogue."

I try not to feel jealous when I see the way Gabriel returns Kie's grin. I try to focus on the deadweight of Rafe in my arms as we haul him back to the van, drive back to Figure 8, and drop his body in the driveway of Tanneyhill so it looks like he made it (almost) home before he passed out.

But it's hard to ignore the tug in my belly, kind of like the feeling I get when I sleep past my alarm and miss Mama's breakfast in the morning. Like I'm too late, and nothing will ever taste so good again.

CHAPTER 27

KIE

"SO *ALAN* WAS THE LAST PERSON TO SEE COLE ALIVE?" GABRIEL asks. "Darren follows Alan around like a puppy. Chances are if Alan was there, Darren wasn't far away."

"We have no reason to believe Darren was there," Pope points out reasonably. "Rafe said he wasn't."

"Rafe lied about Alan!" Gabriel insists. "He lied to his own dad about Alan being there. Why should we believe he isn't lying about Darren, too?"

We're back at the Chateau, strewn across the mix of beat-up lawn furniture and the hammock in the backyard. It's funny, Gabriel's been on the island only a week, but he already seems comfortable here.

What if he decides to stay? What if he becomes a Pogue not just for the night but for real? He could still travel the world to surf, but the OBX could be his home base instead of Brazil.

Then I remember his family back home and the way his expression shifted when he talked about his parents' restaurant. He loves his home. He's not about to leave it behind. Not for me. Not for some girl who wiped out the last time he saw her surf, some girl he hasn't even kissed.

Not that I expect him to kiss me, with everything that's been going on. If we had a window for anything romantic, Cole's death slammed it shut. And I must be the most selfish person in the whole world to be disappointed about that. Like, way to make this tragedy all about *you*, Kiara. If the guys knew I was even thinking about romance at a time like this, I'd never hear the end of it.

I can hear JJ's voice: *Never knew you were so sappy, Kie.*

John B: *Don't be so hard on her, JJ.* Him batting his eyelashes. *The girl's in love.*

JJ, eyes wide with surprise: *Love! You didn't tell us it was love! Tell me, is it going to be a spring wedding?*

It would go on for hours, the other Pogues making fun of me for falling for someone. It's weird, because we have a strict no Pogue-on-Pogue macking policy, but we also can't stand when any of us gets too close to non-Pogues. I know that better than the others. They like to complain that I left them for Kook Academy last year (as if my parents gave me any choice in the matter), but the truth is, when they saw that I was actually making friends with some of my classmates, the guys pulled away from me, not the other way around.

Well, not Pope. I realize that in my fantasy, he isn't making fun of me for falling for Gabriel like JJ and John B.

"Gabriel, I don't trust Rafe as far as I could throw him," John B says, snapping me from my thoughts back into the real world. "But I don't think he was lying to us tonight."

"I don't know, John B, seems like you could throw him pretty far." JJ grins wickedly, snapping open the top of a beer can and taking a swig.

"Let's just be glad he won't remember any of this in the morning. He might remember that it took you and Pope combined to hold him back, and he still almost got away," John B teases.

"That was Pope's fault, not mine!" JJ insists, splashing his beer as he throws out his hands in exasperation. "He's the one who wasn't holding Rafe tight enough." He turns to Pope. "Come to think of it, man, why'd you let him get away so easily?"

"I didn't," Pope says, but I know Pope's voice so well that I can hear the lie. He wasn't holding Rafe tightly on purpose. He didn't want to hurt him. Realizing that makes me love Pope even more than I already do.

Gabriel sits, his head in his hands. "I should feel terrible."

I sit down beside him. "Gabriel, we all know how awful you feel."

Gabriel rakes his hands through his dark hair. "Not about Cole. I already feel awful about Cole. But I should feel terrible that you guys terrorized an innocent kid for me."

At this, JJ and John B burst out laughing. I can't help giggling a little bit, too, and even Pope is smiling.

"Gabriel, I promise you," John B says, "whatever Rafe Cameron is, it's not innocent."

"And even if he was," JJ adds, "I'd do it all over again. We got information out of him. Information he was keeping from the police!"

"Yeah, which is part of why he's not innocent," John B explains. "That's the whole point."

"But I'm saying, even if he was innocent—"

"And I'm saying he wasn't innocent because he was keeping something from the police—"

"Yeah, but I'm saying even if he was—"

Gabriel smiles at me.

"This could take a while," I tell him.

He nods sadly. "I get it. Cole and I could go on like this for hours."

Abruptly, I stand. "Enough!" I shout, loud enough that John B and JJ shut up. "What's next?"

"What do you mean, Kie?" John B asks gently.

"What's our next move in figuring out what really happened to Cole?"

No one says anything for a few minutes. Finally, Pope says, "Okay, what do we know?" He starts pacing as he lists our evidence, one thing after another.

"We know that Cole went missing the day of the contest. We know that his body was found hours later. Thanks to Rafe, we know that Cole was surfing at the Evergreen Bayou early that morning, with no sign of injury or impairment. We know that Alan was there, too. We know that Cole's surfboard was found perfectly intact, his leash attached. We know that Dr. Anderson has listed Cole's official cause of death as drowning."

I put my hands up to stop Pope's pacing. Sometimes when he gets like this, it's almost as if he forgets the rest of us are here. My palms against his chest seems to snap him out of it.

"We know that Cole's phone is missing," Gabriel adds. "It wasn't on the beach or in the motel room."

I nod. "So that's what we know. How about what we don't know?"

"The list of factors we don't know is literally infinite," Pope answers. "We *don't know* what we *don't know*."

"What the hell does that mean?" JJ asks.

"It means that in every investigation there are known unknowns and unknown unknowns," Pope explains. "The known unknowns are the questions we know to ask, the things we know we don't know. But there are an infinite number of factors we don't know we don't know."

JJ rolls his eyes. "I think we've lost Pope to a logic spiral," he moans.

I ignore JJ, holding eye contact with Pope. "Let's focus on the things we *know* we don't know." Now I start pacing. "We don't know whether there was a bump on the back of Cole's head. We don't know whether the marks you saw on his neck were scratches or leash marks. We don't know whether Dr. Anderson made a mistake."

"I've been working with her for weeks!" Pope interjects. "I've literally never seen her make a mistake."

"Okay, then maybe you made a mistake when you said you didn't see a bump on Cole's head and you didn't think the marks on his neck looked like scratches?"

I can practically see Pope's mental struggle. Either his mentor made a mistake or he did—both scenarios that are painfully unlikely as far as he's concerned.

"I don't know!" Pope shouts finally. "I don't know whether to believe Dr. Anderson or what I saw with my own eyes."

"What do we do?" Gabriel asks desperately. "You said Dr. Anderson filed her report and they're cremating Cole's body in the morning."

Pope nods slowly, like his head weighs a hundred pounds. "I don't know," he answers, looking up at the rest of us to see if we have any ideas.

But somehow, the three tiny words seem enormous. Like Pope said, the list of things we don't know is infinite. So really, they're the three biggest words in the world.

CHAPTER 28

POPE

I'M KNOCKING ON A DOOR, BUT NO ONE ANSWERS. MY KNOCK-
ing becomes more and more urgent; I don't know what's on the other side,
but I know I need to get in. I try to twist the doorknob but it's locked. I try to
push my way in, but the door holds fast.

And so I go on knocking, knocking, knocking.

I open my eyes. It was a dream. Not the knocking. The door. The door was
a dream, but the knocking is real.

I don't know what time it was when I came home and crashed onto my bed
without even bothering to take my clothes off. At some point tonight—last
night; it's after midnight now—the five of us all went our separate ways
because it was clear that going around and around in John B's backyard was
getting us nowhere. There was nowhere left to go.

Knock, knock, knock, knock.

I rub the sleep from my eyes and swing my knees over the side of the bed.
Sometimes we get woodpeckers. Dad says you gotta scare them off before
they damage the house too much.

But when woodpeckers target the house, it sounds more like a tap. This is a definite knock.

I turn on the little light beside my bed and almost jump about six feet into the air when I see the shape of a person outlined through my window.

The knocking stops as the person out there starts waving frantically.

Kie.

I get up and open the window.

"What are you doing here? You're gonna wake the whole house with that racket."

"That racket?" Kie echoes, climbing through the window. "What are you, a hundred years old?"

My room is on the second floor, but there's a trellis outside that makes it easy to climb up. Kie, John B, and JJ have used it so often that Dad threatened to take the trellis down, but he never got around to it.

"No, I'm a teenager who was fast asleep about thirty seconds ago, whose parents are just down the hall and definitely won't be okay with me having a girl in my room in the middle of the night."

Kie rolls her eyes. "So it'd be no problem if I were JJ or John B?"

Kie sits on the edge of my bed. I try to remember the last time she was here. I watch her taking in the posters on my A-frame walls, the beat-up telescope I took from our high school when they were going to toss it in favor of a newer version (I thought I could repair it), my rumpled blue sheets, and the pile of clean laundry in the corner, neatly folded by my mother and waiting for me to put it away (Mama says she'll keep my clothes clean, but I'm in charge of keeping them in order).

"I'm not being sexist, Kie."

"And I'm not here to debate the finer points of toxic masculinity—"

"That's a first," I interject, yawning. She'd somehow managed to fit it into Rafe's kidnapping.

"I'm here because I know what we need to do. And we need to do it now, tonight. This minute."

Kie stands and paces from one end of my room to the other. She wrings her hands. Her hair is wild around her face, her curls sticking out in all directions. I've never seen her look so nervous.

"Whatever it is, Kie, we'll do it." I try to sound composed, grown up. Like my dad did when I used to have bad dreams and he'd come into this room to calm me down. "Tell me what we need to do."

Finally, Kie stops moving.

"We need to break into the morgue."

CHAPTER 29

POPE

I TRIED TO BE REASONABLE. I TOLD KIE I COULD LOSE MY JOB. I told her it was trespassing and very much illegal. I reminded her that the morgue is literally underneath the police station, so we'd be breaking the law within literal earshot of the men and women whose job is to catch people breaking the law.

But Kie won out in the end. Maybe I always knew she would. I've never been able to say no to her.

And it's not just that, and maybe Kie knew it, too. I need to know whether I really missed a bump on Cole's head or imagined the leash marks around his neck. I have to get this right. Not just for me. For Gabriel, too. Even if I don't like how close Kie stands to him, I also can't help feeling for the guy. He just wants to find out what happened to his best friend. I'd do the same thing for Kie, for John B, for JJ. And, as much as I hate to admit it, there's something about Gabriel. It's hard not to like him. Pop never opened up to John B or JJ the way he did to Gabriel. He's never opened up to *me* that way.

Which is why I'm crouched in the seagrass surrounding the police station, ready to break into the morgue in the middle of the night.

Kie's not wrong. Once they take Cole's body away in the morning, there goes our biggest piece of evidence. I can't argue with logic that sound.

"There," I whisper-shout, seeing a cracked window on the first floor.

"Do you have any idea what room is attached to that window?" Kie asks reasonably.

"No clue," I admit. "But can you think of a better way in?"

Every day for work, I walk directly into the precinct lobby and head down the stairs to the morgue. There's one door that leads directly to the basement from outside that is used for delivering and removing bodies, but it's firmly locked and protected by an alarm on top of that. The only way in is through the station.

"There could be someone in there," Gabriel points out. "We could get caught before we've gotten anywhere."

Both Kie and Gabriel are making good points, logical points. The sort of things that, under normal circumstances, I'm the one saying to try to keep John B and JJ and even Kie from going haywire. But it's equally as logical to conclude that the open window is our only way in.

"I'm sorry we got you into this, Pope," Kie whispers as we crouch-walk toward the window.

"You didn't get me into anything."

"There's no reason for anyone other than Gabriel and me to be here, to be taking this risk."

"I'm the only one who knows his way around the coroner's office," I point out.

"I know," Kie says, her voice heavy, like she wouldn't have brought me with her here tonight if she could've thought of another way.

"Way to make a guy feel wanted, Kie."

"That's not what I mean," Kie insists. "I just don't want to get you into trouble. I know how much the internship means to you."

Kie reaches out and squeezes my hand. Unlike John B and JJ, she's never made fun of my career choices, and she appreciates what I'm putting on the line tonight. I remember how it felt a few days ago when Kie yelled at me, that terrible feeling like the one person who understands me best might have hated me, even just for a few minutes. I would do anything for Kie, even risk my career, because there's nothing more important than a person who really *gets* you.

We're directly beneath the window. It's now or never.

"If we get caught tonight, I'll have gotten *myself* into trouble, not you," I tell Kie, then heave myself up.

Luckily, there's no one waiting on the other side of the window. It's an empty office that must belong to an officer who works the day shift, someone who forgot to close their window before leaving at the end of the day. The office is dark, but its walls are made of glass, so there's no chance of hiding out here. We have to keep moving.

"Come on," I say, leaning out the window to give Gabriel, then Kie, an arm up.

"Step one complete," Kie says triumphantly, closing the window behind her.

As soon as the window clicks shut, a screeching sound fills the air, so loud I cover my ears.

"Let's get out of here!" Gabriel says, grabbing Kie's wrist as he pulls her out the office door.

"Who'd've thought *closing* a window would set off the alarm?" Kie shouts to be heard over the wailing sound. At least we don't have to worry that someone will hear us.

We race down the hall and around the corner, eager to get as far from the source of the alarm as possible, and fall into a crouch and wait, chests heaving and hearts thumping.

I hear footsteps coming from the other direction, racing toward the office we just left behind. I put a hand over my mouth, indicating that Kie and Gabriel should stay quiet.

The alarm stops. "Foley's office," I hear someone say. "He mentioned his alarm had been glitchy."

"Leave a note for him to call maintenance in the morning."

I hear papers shuffling. I guess one of the officers is leaving a note on Foley's desk.

Then the sound of the door closing, footsteps moving. I wait for them to fade away as the officers go back the way they came, but instead they get louder and louder.

Shit, they're coming right toward us.

"What do we do?" Kie whispers.

I shake my head frantically, but Gabriel stands. "I got this," he says with a smile, and starts walking toward the officers.

"Oh, thank goodness," he says. "I feel like I've been wandering around this place for hours."

"What are you doing here?" one of the officers asks. He's in uniform, but even though it's the middle of the night, a pair of sunglasses is perched on top of his head. "You can't be back here."

"Sorry," Gabriel says quickly, "but my dog is missing. We came in to file a report." He gestures to Kie and me. "The guy at the front desk told us to make a left and then a right, and then we heard that alarm and freaked out . . ."

"We got lost," Kie finishes. "We're so sorry."

I hold my breath, waiting for the officers to poke holes in Gabriel's story, but instead, their faces soften.

"I'd be going nuts if my pup went missing," Sunglasses says. "What's his name?"

"Cole," Kie answers, just as Gabriel says, "Surfboard."

"Surfboard," Gabriel repeats. "Cole's a nickname."

"Cute name," the softhearted officer says. "Mine's Chewy." He holds out his phone to show us a picture.

"Looks like a nice dog," I stammer.

"Do you have any pictures of Cole?" No Glasses asks, all business.

Smooth as silk, Gabriel pulls his phone out of his pocket and brings up a picture of a small, wiry-haired white dog.

"That's a handsome boy," Sunglasses says with a smile. "I hope you find him."

Gabriel makes a pained face. Kie reaches up and strokes his arm reassuringly. How are they so good at this while I'm standing here tongue-tied?

"Well, you better get going," No Glasses adds finally. He points in the direction from which he came. "You can file a report with Tom up front."

"Thanks!" Gabriel says, and starts moving like he's in a terrible hurry. "Not a minute to waste."

Kie and I hurry after him. We wait until the officers round the corner.

"How did you just happen to have a picture of the perfect dog on your phone?"

Gabriel shrugs. "That's my dog back home in Brazil."

"Is his name really Surfboard?"

"In Portuguese."

How does Gabriel look cool even here in the police station in the middle of the night, moments after we were nearly caught and kicked out? He smiles his wide, friendly smile and says, "Lead the way, Pope," reminding me that I'm the only one who knows the way down to the morgue. It's almost enough to make me feel cool, too.

And so I lead the way.

CHAPTER 30

KIE

I CAN'T HELP IT. I CLOSE MY EYES WHEN POPE OPENS THE drawer—is *drawer* the right word for it?—with Cole's body inside.

I know this is the right thing to do, the only way to give Gabriel peace of mind, but somehow it *feels* wrong. It feels like something out of a horror movie. You know, the scene where the unsuspecting kids go into the basement instead of running out the front door. Because here we are, in the basement of a dangerous building surrounded by dead bodies. And no one knows we're here. Pope and I agreed that we weren't going to tell JJ and John B until we got the job done, because otherwise they'd have insisted on coming with us, and the more of us here, the greater our chances of getting caught. Subtlety isn't exactly JJ's strong suit. John B's either, for that matter.

So no one knows we're here. And now Pope is opening what he says is called a "mortuary cabinet," those cold metal doors with cold metal tables that slide out from inside with cold dead bodies lying on top of them.

I can hear the table being pulled out of the cabinet, can hear the sharp breath Gabriel inhales when Pope pulls the sheet back, revealing Gabriel's best friend's body.

Stop being a baby, Kie. I open my eyes.

And there he is. The saddest, strangest thing is that he doesn't look that different from the day I met him. Except, of course, he looks completely different. His lips aren't parted in a smile so wide you can see most of his gleaming white teeth. His blond hair isn't blowing in the breeze off the ocean. His eyes aren't open, squinting in the sunlight. It hits me that I can't remember what color his eyes are. Which, on any normal day, wouldn't seem like such a big deal. Why should I remember the color of some guy's eyes when I met him only a couple of times? But right now, it seems really, really important. I remember his order at The Wreck: fried clams, extra tartar sauce, cold beer. He winked when he ordered the beer, like he could tell I'm not the kind of waitress who asks for ID unless my dad is watching.

How come I can remember something as unimportant as his dinner order but not the color of his eyes?

Thinking about The Wreck makes me feel queasy. I haven't been to work in days. I've been sneaking in the house after I know Mom and Dad are sleeping—even when they try to wait up, they can't make it that late. And then I leave before they get up in the morning. Tonight, I was barely home long enough to take a shower and change my clothes—my tank top and cutoffs need to be de-Rafed in the washing machine, ew—before I made my way across the island from our house in Figure 8 to Pope's place in the Cut.

I'll explain it to my parents eventually, how important it was for me to be here for my friends. For Gabriel. They'll never understand, but I'll tell them anyway. They'll use it as an excuse to send me back to Kook Academy, but I won't go. On the first day of class, I'm walking through the public school doors alongside my friends no matter what my parents say. They'll have to drag me out kicking and screaming, and Mom and Dad don't like that kind of scene.

The hypocrisy is the worst part. Like their insistence that the Pogues are a bad influence. As if they don't know that the Kooks throw parties and stay out too late and use substances they're not supposed to. At least the Pogues are honest about it.

"He looks so small," Gabriel murmurs. "He's taller than me, I know he is, but he looks so small."

I put my hand on Gabriel's back. I can feel the way he's shuddering with every breath, like he's trying not to cry. It's cold in here, but I can feel the warmth of Gabriel's skin under his t-shirt.

"How does he look so small?" Gabriel asks, turning from his friend to face me. "I never believed in, I don't know, God and souls and stuff, but do you think, when he died, whatever part of him that was Cole left his body, so that there's literally less of him here?" He gestures at the metal slab.

"Maybe." I nod slowly. "I don't know what I believe, either."

Gabriel leans against me, his body warm against mine. He puts his arm around me, and suddenly his embrace twists into a hug. I wait for Pope to launch into some kind of technical explanation. For all I know, dead bodies weigh less than live ones. Like, if the human body is sixty percent water, maybe some of that water leaves the body when you die, like evaporates over time so that you shrink.

I look at Pope, trying to silently communicate that now isn't the time for a scientific explanation, but he already seems to understand it, his mouth firmly shut in a straight line.

"Okay," Gabriel says, letting me go. "Let's get on with it."

"Get on with it?" I echo. For a second, I forget why we're here, even though this whole thing was my brilliant plan in the first place.

"Right," Pope agrees. He turns on a light overhead, almost like a spotlight, the kind you see in operating rooms on TV shows about doctors who spend more time dealing with personal problems than actually treating patients. Mom loves those shows.

I don't know if Cole is any smaller than he used to be, but to me, he looks paler. Like only a few days out of the sun, in this windowless basement, was enough to rob him of his tan. Pope shines the light on Cole's upper body. I can see red marks snaking around his neck. Without thinking, without remembering that this is a dead body and I'm scared of dead bodies, I lean down to get a closer look.

"What do you think, Kie?" Pope asks. I snap back up.

"You're the expert, Pope, not me."

"Yeah, but what do you think?"

"I don't think they look like scratches."

"What do they look like?"

Gabriel answers for me. "It looks like something was wrapped around his neck. Tight."

Pope nods his head in heavy agreement. "It just doesn't make sense to me," he murmurs. "How could Dr. Anderson miss something like that?"

Pope is the sort of person who believes that every question has an answer, like a key fitting into a lock. He thinks that he can figure out every single one of life's mysteries if he can sit in a library long enough to do the research and talk to experts and apply logic and reason.

This is the first time I've seen him express any doubt that there could be a reasonable explanation.

"Let's check his head," Gabriel suggests.

"His head?" I echo, but Pope's already shifting the spotlight and turning Cole's neck to the side to get a better look. He's wearing latex gloves, and he handles Cole's body gently, respectfully, as though Cole might still be able to feel his touch.

It makes me want to give him a hug as big as the one Gabriel just gave me.

"Nothing," Pope says, shaking his head incredulously. "You can see, around his mouth, a bit of a bruise and swelling from where Darren punched him at The Wreck."

My stomach twists at the mention of the restaurant.

"But," Pope continues, "that's the only sign of any sort of injury—"

"Other than the marks around his neck," Gabriel finishes.

"Exactly," Pope agrees.

"It had to be Darren," Gabriel says firmly. "He could've easily overheard JJ telling Cole about the local spot the day they met at The Wreck. Or he could've just been there with Alan that morning."

"But Rafe said Darren wasn't there," I point out gently.

"So maybe he got there after Rafe left. Who else could it have been? The police should at least call him in for questioning. There are tons of eyewitnesses who saw them fighting just days before Cole showed up dead."

"They're not going to call anyone in for questioning, now that the death was ruled an accident," Pope explains.

"This wasn't an accident!" Gabriel shouts, pointing at his best friend's neck. You can see that, can't you, Pope?"

"I don't know. Honestly, I don't. I think we have to ask more questions."

"Yeah," I agree, recalling the conversation I overheard at Gabriel's motel. "And we have to ask them before Alan whisks Darren off to Costa Rica for his next competition."

CHAPTER 31

POPE

"IT JUST DOESN'T MAKE ANY SENSE." I STEP AWAY FROM THE table, leaving Kie and Gabriel standing over Cole's body while I pace back and forth, trying to work this out.

It's cold in here, but then it's always cold in here. I didn't turn on the fluorescent lights overhead, only the spotlight over Cole's body. I know some people would find this room spooky, but I never did. The morgue is no creepier than anyplace else. Bodies don't suddenly become sinister the minute they stop breathing. But something about being here tonight, when I'm not supposed to be here, with the spotlight casting its bright glare across Cole's body—the body that maybe died in a different way from how Dr. Anderson says it died—feels spooky, creepy, strange, wrong.

I shake my head. That's magical thinking, not logic. Cole's body isn't unlike any other body. He's not going to sit up and announce who killed him. Still, his body can tell us exactly how he died. That's not magic; it's science.

"What doesn't make sense, Pope?" Kie asks.

"Every question has a logical explanation. Every mystery, a scientific solution." Why the waves do what they do, why the Northern Lights sparkle across the sky, why ships are more likely to get lost in the Bermuda Triangle. For centuries, human beings attributed these sorts of phenomena to spirits and witchcraft, but after thousands of years, we have scientific explanations, and the science always wins out.

And if there's a reasonable explanation for enormous questions like those, then there's a reasonable explanation for why Dr. A listed Cole's cause of death as drowning.

"It must have been a mistake," I begin.

"You're always saying how good Dr. Anderson is at her job," Kie reminds me.

"Everyone has a bad day," I suggest, but the explanation rings hollow.

"Bad enough to rule the cause of death as drowning when it's obviously strangulation?" Kie prompts, saying out loud exactly what I'm thinking, like she's the voice in my head, debating magical thinking versus logical explanations.

In the Sherlock Holmes mysteries, Sir Arthur Conan Doyle wrote, "When you have eliminated the impossible, whatever remains, however improbable, must be the truth."

Scientific Question: How do you explain a mistake your mentor would never make?

215

Hypothesis: If your mentor would never make such a mistake, then maybe it wasn't a mistake at all.

I stop pacing abruptly. "Why would Dr. Anderson lie?" I ask, my voice almost a whisper.

"What?" Kie says.

"It's the only logical conclusion," I explain. "Dr. Anderson's covering up Cole's cause of death."

"Can't she get into, like, really big trouble for that?"

"Yeah," I say, nodding. "She would lose her job, her medical license, even go to prison."

"Why would she risk all that?"

"I don't know." I start pacing again. "Maybe Darren offered to give her the money he won in the competition?"

Dr. Anderson makes a good living as county coroner, but maybe she's in debt or something. Maybe she has a gambling addiction and owes money to the Mob, and hit men are going to break her fingers if she doesn't pay up, so she risked her medical license for the money. With her hands destroyed, it's not like she'd be able to do her job anymore.

I shake my head. That's ridiculous. It's the plot to a bad movie, not real life.

"There was a phone call," I say suddenly.

"What phone call?" Kie asks.

"Right after we started Cole's exam, Dr. A's phone rang. She said she had to go, and then the next morning when I got in, she'd completed the exam before I got here. She went from recognizing the leash marks for what they are to calling them scratches."

Gabriel pulls the sheet over Cole's body and turns on his heel. "Let's go," he says.

"Where?"

"Upstairs. To the police. We need to file a report. Tell them what we found and about your boss."

"No way," I say.

"Why not?" Gabriel's voice drops an octave. "You protecting your boss?"

There's a hint of a threat in the question.

"No!" I insist. "But the police aren't going to believe us over her."

"But we have all this evidence!" Gabriel gestures to his friend's body.

"We need a better plan," I say.

"I'm tired of waiting. Cole deserves better." Gabriel heads for the stairwell. I follow, desperate to stop him.

Gabriel reaches the door at the top of the stairs, his hand on the handle.

But the handle doesn't turn. For a second, I think Gabriel has changed his mind.

"What the hell?" Gabriel shakes the handle.

"Let me try," Kie offers, reaching for the door.

"Kie, don't!" I whisper-shout.

But when Kie tries, the door doesn't budge.

"It must've locked from the other side when we came down here," I say. "No one comes to the morgue overnight, not unless there's a body to drop off."

"So you're saying we're trapped down here until Dr. Anderson shows up in the morning?" Kie shudders, and I realize she didn't try to open the door to help Gabriel, but because she was scared of being down here.

I nod firmly. "Yes, Kie. We're trapped down here."

CHAPTER 32

KIE

I'VE NEVER THOUGHT OF MYSELF AS A WIMP. I TAKE TO THE water just as aggressively as JJ, if with a little bit more thought and care. I can hold my liquor (almost) as well as John B. And even though I don't care about school as much as Pope does, I don't wither under a tough assignment from our teachers. I'm not the kind of girl who plays damsel in distress to get a guy's attention. It would've been easy to get Rafe that way earlier, to pretend I'd had too much to drink and needed some fresh air. But that's not my style.

So it's hard for me to admit, tonight, that I'm scared.

I'm not scared because we're locked in the basement of a police station and could be discovered and arrested at any moment. I don't doubt my ability to argue our case to the cops, even though they might not believe me. They probably wouldn't listen well enough anyway.

Gabriel sinks to the ground beneath Cole's body, like he doesn't want to put any distance between himself and his friend. It's so sweet and sad. And the look on Gabriel's face: like no one could make him move away from his friend until the truth gets out. I should sit down beside him in solidarity, but I find myself backing away. One step, then another.

I'm scared of spending a night in the morgue, surrounded by dead bodies.

"Hey!" Pope whisper-shouts as I back right over his foot.

"Sorry!" I spin around.

"Since when are you so clumsy?" Pope asks.

"I'm not," I answer quickly. "It's just . . ." I pause. Pope won't understand. Pope wants to spend the rest of his life in rooms like these.

"I get it," Pope says, surprising me.

"You do?"

"It's the middle of the night. It's dark. It's cold. And you're trapped in a room filled with dead bodies."

"Filled?" I echo, looking at the mortuary cabinets that line the walls. "Is it really filled?"

Pope shakes his head. "Figure of speech," he says, though he doesn't tell me how many dead bodies—other than Cole's—are down here.

"I thought you'd tell me I'm being ridiculous."

"I'd never call you ridiculous," Pope says solemnly, and something about the way he's looking at me makes me want to look away.

"It's just . . ." I drop my whisper even lower. I don't want Gabriel to hear. ". . . it doesn't look like he's sleeping."

"Huh?"

"You know how they say that dead people look like they're asleep or something? Cole doesn't look like he's sleeping."

I can't explain it. He's lying down; his eyes are closed. But somehow, you can tell. It's not just the pallor of his skin, though he looks several shades paler than he did the day I met him in the sunshine. Like Gabriel said, Cole looks somehow *smaller*. I don't know what I believe about spirits and souls and all that, but Cole looks like something is missing, some fundamental piece that's the difference between being alive and being dead. And without that missing piece, there's no way anyone would think he was asleep. And that's the scary part. I don't think Cole's going to, like, rise from the dead and haunt us. But there's something so chilling about seeing a body without that missing piece.

"It's *creepy*, being this close to a dead body," I say finally.

"Don't think of it that way," Pope says gently.

"How else can I think about it?"

"We're watching over Cole. Taking care of him. Protecting him. Wouldn't you want to be watched over by a friend, if it were you on that table?"

Pope nods in the direction of Cole's dead body, and I picture myself lying there instead of Cole; I try to imagine myself without whatever pieces of me are most alive.

"I didn't mean to talk about your dead body," Pope stammers, mistaking my silence for disgust. "In some cultures, it's tradition to watch over the

deceased before burial or cremation. Jewish people have a name for it—
shemira, the ritual of watching over a body from death until burial. A male
guardian is called a *shomer*, and a female guardian is a *shomeret*—"

"I know what you meant," I cut in quickly. When Pope's nervous, he fills
the silence with all the facts and figures he's learned. "How'd you know
that, anyway?"

"When I got this internship, I studied the mourning rituals of a bunch of
different cultures. I wanted to make sure I treated every person who passed
through here with respect."

I smile. I've known Pope so long that sometimes I think I've gotten used to
what a good person he is. But every so often, his goodness still manages to
surprise me.

"You're right," I say softly.

"About what?"

"If it were me, I'd want you to be here, watching over me. I mean, I guess
I wouldn't want anything anymore, I'd be dead, but—"

"I know what you meant," Pope says, and he smiles.

"Thanks," I say.

"For what?"

"For making me feel better about being trapped down here."

"Any time."

I grin. "Well, let's hope this doesn't become a habit."

I mean for it to be a joke, but Pope looks sad. "I'm pretty sure I'm not going to be allowed down here after this evening."

"I know how much you risked for Gabriel tonight."

"I didn't do it for Gabriel," Pope says solemnly, and again there's something in the way he looks at me that makes it hard to maintain eye contact. Quickly, Pope adds, "I did it for Cole, of course. For his family. For all of his friends, not just Gabriel. They deserve to know what really happened to him."

"Yeah," I agree, looking across the room at Gabriel. I'm not sure I've ever seen another human being look so sad. "They do."

I swallow my fear and take one step, then another. Like Pope said, we're here to watch over Cole. All of us, not Gabriel alone.

"Hey," I whisper, finally sinking onto the floor beside Gabriel. I think I'd whisper even if we weren't in the basement of the police station. Something about being here feels sacred.

"Hey," Gabriel answers.

"You okay?" I ask.

I'm sitting close enough that I can feel Gabriel's shoulders shrug. "I honestly don't know."

"Me, either."

I don't think I've ever been so cold. I'm wearing shorts and a cropped tank—perfect for the humid weather outside, but not ideal for this room. My hair's twisted into a bun on the top of my head. I release it, letting my hair fall onto my bare shoulders like a scarf.

"You're shivering," Gabriel says. He shifts, and then his arm is around me. He's not dressed any more warmly than I am—he and Pope are both wearing t-shirts and shorts—but somehow his skin is warm against mine.

"Pope said they keep the AC in this room set to sixty degrees," I explain.

"I guess they have to," Gabriel says.

"Yeah, I guess."

Gabriel tightens his hold on me, and I burrow closer, curling into a ball.

I know Pope said he'd never call me ridiculous, but right now, I feel completely absurd. Because here I am, sitting on the cold linoleum floor of a morgue, trapped below the police station, Gabriel's best friend's body lying on a table just a few feet above us, and I feel . . . I don't know. This has got to be the least romantic place on Earth, but somehow, I feel like Gabriel wants to kiss me. Not here, not now—he would never do that. But I'm suddenly certain that someday, when all of this is over, he's going to.

And that certainty makes me warm all over.

"We should try to get some sleep," Pope says, sitting down on the other side of me. He keeps a few inches between his body and mine, careful not to touch me.

I nod, but I know there's no way I'm going to sleep here, not with Cole's body hovering over us.

After a few minutes, Gabriel's arms grow heavy around me, and I know he's falling asleep. Pope's breaths became steady and shallow. I wonder if they're dreaming. I wonder what they're dreaming.

I find myself thinking about John B, alone at the Chateau for yet another night, wondering when his dad will come home. None of us know what happened to Big John, but we know, after all these months, it's unlikely that wherever he is, he's alive and well. None of us has ever said it out loud. I'm not sure what John B would say if one of us did.

When I close my eyes, I picture Big John out there on the water, alone. Maybe he got thrown from his boat and drowned; maybe he ran out of water. It's crazy to think about dehydration in the middle of the ocean. *Water, water, everywhere, and not a drop to drink.* Whatever happened, he was probably alone. There was no one to watch over him. No one to sit vigil.

I don't feel frightened anymore. I sit up a bit straighter, so that I can make out Cole's profile.

"Don't worry," I tell him. "You're not alone. We're watching over you."

CHAPTER 33

POPE

THE SOUND OF A KEY IN THE LOCK MAKES ALL THREE OF US jump to our feet. I check my phone; it's just after eight a.m. Dr. Anderson hardly has her foot in the door before Gabriel is shouting at her.

"Why did you falsify the autopsy?"

Dr. Anderson looks from Gabriel to Kie, then to me. Her eyes soften for a second, like she's relieved to see a familiar face, then harden into a defensive stance. I guess I can't blame her after the accusation Gabriel just hurled.

"Pope, who are these people?"

"These are my friends—" I begin, but Dr. Anderson doesn't let me finish.

"And you thought it would be fun to sneak your friends into the morgue at the crack of dawn? How did you guys get down here, anyway?"

Dr. Anderson strides across the room, taking her white coat off the hook by the door as she moves. She puts her bag on the floor and a cup of coffee on an empty shelf, then pulls her phone from her bag and slips it into the pocket of her coat, just as I've seen her do every morning all summer.

She takes a sip of her coffee. "Need I remind you, Pope, that our patients have been entrusted to us by their families and the police investigating their demise. To see you treating this space with such disrespect, all to give your friends some kind of thrill—"

"It's not like that!" I jump in, but Dr. Anderson continues as if I haven't spoken.

"I can only assume this is the result of a one-time lapse in judgment, since it seems so very out of character with the young man I've gotten to know this summer."

Dr. Anderson looks at me meaningfully. It takes me a moment to realize exactly what she's saying. If I leave now, quietly, with Kie and Gabriel, she won't report me to the officers upstairs. I can continue to work here for the rest of the summer. She'll still write me a letter of recommendation.

It occurs to me that Dr. Anderson hasn't denied Gabriel's accusation.

For once, I don't give myself a chance to think before I take action. I spring across the room, pulling the doctor's phone from her pocket. I'm certain that whatever Dr. Anderson did, it all started with the phone call she got the morning Cole's body arrived.

"What are you doing?" Dr. Anderson shouts as I hold the phone up to her face to unlock it. She reaches for me, spilling coffee everywhere. I shout when the hot liquid hits my bare arm, but I hold the phone up so it won't get drenched. Kie lunges across the room, blocking the doctor.

I scroll through the recent calls until I find the right one: Tuesday morning, 10:11 a.m.

"It says it's from Al," I say.

"Al?" asks Kie.

"Yeah, Al."

I call the number, and a man's voice answers on the second ring. "Everything all set, little sis?"

Kie, Gabriel, and I all lock eyes. We know that voice.

I hang up the phone as everything clicks for me at once. My dad's memories of Alan competing on the beaches of OBX. Dr. A growing up around here, just a few towns over.

Dr. Elizabeth Anderson.

Née Thomas.

Little sis.

Alan and Dr. Anderson are brother and sister.

✳ ✳ ✳

GABRIEL LETS OUT A SHORT, HUMORLESS LAUGH THAT SOUNDS more like a bark. "Al. Alan Thomas. I can't believe this."

"See?" Kie shouts. "He's covering up for his star client."

I look at Dr. Anderson. She doesn't answer, but her gaze shifts to Cole's body, lying on the mortuary cabinet table.

Just then, there's the sound of a key turning in the lock on the door—not the door that leads up into the police station, but the one that leads directly outside. Two large white men walk inside; they're wearing dark brown coveralls emblazoned with "Kildare Funeral Home," their names, Roy and Eddie, sewn neatly beneath the company logo.

They're here for Cole's body.

That's what Alan meant by "all set."

He meant: *Has the evidence been destroyed?*

"No!" I shout, and I fling myself across the room, planting my feet in front of Cole. Kie springs for Dr. Anderson like she's worried the doctor might make a run for it.

"We're here to pick up . . ." One of the two men looks at a clipboard in his hands and reads, "Cole Johnson."

"Help!" Dr. Anderson shouts. "Help!"

A police officer comes scrambling down the stairs from the station above. "What seems to be the problem, Liz?" he asks.

"These kids broke into the morgue overnight. They're trying to steal a body."

The officer's eyes widen. "What kind of sick—"

"We're not trying to steal anything," I shout. "Please! You can't let them cremate Cole."

The officer crosses the room. I realize he's headed straight for Kie, since she's the one who's restraining Dr. Anderson. He pulls out a pair of hand-cuffs and wrenches Kie's hand from Dr. Anderson, slamming the metal onto one of Kie's wrists. I hear the mechanism slide into the lock.

"No!" Gabriel shouts, rushing the police officer so that he loses his balance before he can cuff Kie's other wrist. The officer stumbles, bumping into the mortuary cabinet table. When he falls, he takes the sheet covering Cole's body down with him.

"Look!" I yell, gesturing wildly at Roy and Eddie, the men from the funeral home. They see dead bodies every day; maybe they can help us. "Please look at his neck."

"This is ridiculous," Dr. Anderson says, but her voice is shaking. "I examined the body myself!" She yanks the sheet out from under the police officer who attempted to arrest Kie and tries to place it over Cole's body. Roy stops her, holding the sheet back.

"There are leash marks on the boy's neck," he says, bending down to look more closely. He refers to his clipboard. "This says the cause of death was drowning, not strangulation." He nods to his partner. "Eddie, take a look."

"This is all a misunderstanding," Dr. Anderson says. "My intern is a bit overenthusiastic—"

"Your intern recognized the marks the day they brought Cole's body in," Kie says, rubbing her wrist where the officer cuffed her. "You expect us to believe that with all your years of medical school and experience, you missed something that a high schooler saw right away?" Kie pauses, then adds, "Even if he is the smartest high schooler this island's ever seen."

I can't help it. Despite everything else, I feel myself swelling with pride under Kie's praise.

"I didn't miss anything," Dr. Anderson says through gritted teeth.

The officer makes his way up to stand. "If you didn't miss anything, Liz," he says, "then why does the report say this boy drowned, when Eddie and Roy—and your intern—say he was strangled?"

CHAPTER 34

KIE

GABRIEL'S BREATHING HEAVY, LIKE HE'S JUST RUN A MARA-
thon, even though rushing that officer was barely enough to make him break
a sweat. His jaw is clenched and his eyes go wide, like he's just figured something out.

I hear screeching brakes from outside, which means John B and JJ are
pulling up in the Twinkie. They must have figured out where we are. Gabriel
makes a face like he's plotting something.

Before I know it, he's running—past the police officer and the guys from
the funeral home, past Pope and Dr. Anderson and me.

He runs straight through the door the funeral home guys walked through
a few moments ago. I wait for half a second, then turn on my heel and follow,
even though the officer's cuffs are still hanging from my left wrist.

It doesn't take much time before Pope is running behind us.

Gabriel kicks off his flip-flops and I do the same; they're only slowing us
down. Like mine, Gabriel's feet are tough and calloused from years of

walking barefoot on the beach, holding his stance on a surfboard. We all make it to the Twinkie, pile in, and John B hits the gas.

"That's the last time you guys don't fill us in on a plan," John B growls as he twists the steering wheel. JJ scoffs in agreement.

I roll my eyes, even though I know he's right. "Thanks for coming, guys. We'll get there in time," I say, even though no one has actually confirmed where we're going. But we don't have to. We already know.

Darren and Alan are leaving for Costa Rica today. They could already be on the ferry, headed to the mainland and then to the airport after that. They could be out of town—out of the country—before the police can arrest them.

They could get away with everything.

I pull my phone from my pocket as we careen up to the ferry landing. It's 8:17 a.m. The first ferry to the mainland leaves at 8:30. The Twinkie is still moving when I wrench open the door and tumble out, Pope and Gabriel on my heels. "We'll hang back in case you guys need a getaway," John B says as we start toward the dock.

"Don't do anything I wouldn't do," JJ calls after us.

There's a line of people waiting to get onto the ferry. Plenty of people take it every day, to get to jobs they have on the mainland. Darren stands out in the crowd in his board shorts and flip-flops; so does Alan in his suit.

Neither of them sees Pope and Gabriel, both slightly ahead of me, coming.

They grab Darren so hard he loses his balance. All three of them topple to the ground.

"What the hell?" Darren shouts.

"Stop!" I shout, just as loud. I run right past Darren and the guys, pouncing on Alan like a cat. He spins around, but I lock my legs around his waist, like a child who doesn't want to be put down after a piggyback ride. I can feel the heat of his body radiating beneath me. Who wears a wool suit in the summertime?

Gabriel and Pope are holding Darren on the ground, the wooden planks of the dock splintering beneath him.

"Don't!" I shout. "It wasn't Darren." The conversation I overheard at the motel clicks in my brain. I'd misunderstood.

"What do you mean it wasn't Darren?" Gabriel's panting as Darren tries to fight him off.

"Darren wanted to stay in town," I explain. "I heard them talking. He didn't care about winning or leaving or surfing. I'd thought it was . . . something else. But now I realize he was actually sad about what happened to Cole." Alan writhes beneath me, trying to throw me off, but I hold firm. "*Alan*'s the one who was pushing him to leave."

He didn't call his little sister to cover up for his star client. He called her to cover up for *himself*.

"Get off me, you crazy kid!" Alan shouts. He throws his arms out, at last managing to shake me off, but I turn my body so that I won't fall on my back, landing lightly on my feet instead.

Alan starts to run, but I throw a leg out, tripping him. I slow him down, but he manages to find his footing, taking off again.

"Help!" I shout. Gabriel hesitates, but Pope moves fast. He releases his grip on Darren and chases Alan. After a beat, Gabriel does the same. Suddenly free, Darren looks shell-shocked.

Alan's heading for the ferry, parked by the side of the dock. No, he's running toward the edge of the dock, so fast that for a second I think he's going to jump right off it and attempt to swim to the mainland.

I get to my feet and start running after Alan, Pope, and Gabriel. Alan's rapidly approaching the edge of the dock and reaching into his pocket. He's faster than I would've guessed, in his suit and fancy shoes. He tosses whatever's in his pocket into the air.

Footsteps are pounding behind me; Darren quickly overtakes me, then Gabriel, then Pope. He runs right past Alan and leaps into the air, as agile on dry land as he is in the water. He catches what Alan tossed before it can go over the end of the dock and into the ocean.

The sound of sirens fills the air, followed by car doors opening and slamming shut, police officers running up the dock.

"Thank goodness you're here!" Alan shouts, out of breath. "These kids came out of nowhere and attacked me."

Two officers head down the dock, straight for Gabriel, Pope, Alan, and me. Or, at least, I think they're headed for us, but then they reach for Alan instead.

"Alan Thomas, you are under arrest for the murder of Cole Johnson."

"This is preposterous," Alan begins, but the officers continue, reading off his Miranda rights just like they do in the movies, their hands on his shoulders.

"Your sister confessed," one of the officers explains. "She's cutting a deal as we speak. She may have been willing to lose her license for you, but she wasn't about to go to prison."

Pope looks crushed. I think he was still holding out hope that his mentor might have been one of the good guys.

"Can someone please tell me what the hell is going on?" Darren shouts.

"Your manager is a sleazeball," Pope explains, which only makes Darren look more confused.

"He murdered my best friend so that you'd win the contest," Gabriel says.

Darren shakes his head. "No way. Why would he kill someone for three thousand dollars?"

"Three thousand dollars?" Gabriel echoes.

"Yeah, that's his cut of my prize winnings. Ten percent of thirty K."

"Leave it to you to nickel-and-dime a murder." Gabriel sounds disgusted.

"I didn't mean it like that!" Darren insists. "I just meant—this doesn't make any sense."

He's still gripping whatever it was that Alan tried to toss into the ocean. I look more closely.

"Whose phone is that?" I ask.

Gabriel lunges across the dock, ripping the phone from Darren's hands.

"That's Cole's phone," he says. "I recognize the case. Why would Alan want to destroy Cole's phone?"

"Because it'd look suspicious if he had it?" I suggest.

Gabriel turns back to Darren. "Why'd you lunge for it?" he asks suspiciously.

"'Cause I figured it was important, the way Alan was trying to get rid of it."

"Gabriel," I suggest, "if Darren had anything to do with this, he'd have wanted Alan to get rid of the phone, right?"

Gabriel turns the phone on, but it's password protected.

"I know his password." Gabriel types in a series of numbers. The phone opens to an audio recording. Gabriel presses play, turning the volume up as loud as it goes.

A man's voice fills the air.

"See you later, Cameron. Sorry we couldn't work anything out."

"That's Alan's voice," Darren says.

"Yeah, you will be sorry!"

"That's Rafe," Pope supplies. He looks at the time stamp on the recording. "This is from the morning of the tow-in contest. Rafe said when he left the Evergreen Bayou, Cole and Alan were still there. This must be right after Alan said he wouldn't represent Rafe."

Alan's voice speaks again. *"Let's go over the deal again."*

"Throw the competition today, win in Costa Rica so no one gets suspicious, then throw in Fiji and the North Shore."

237

"That's Cole!" Gabriel shouts.

Alan's voice: *"That's right."*

Cole's: *"Remind me why I'm doing this again? The purses for these contests aren't major."*

Alan's: *"Yeah, but the endorsement deals that come from that many wins are. Don't worry. You'll get your cut."*

"No way would Cole agree to this," Gabriel says, but Cole starts talking.

"I wanted to discuss that part of the deal again. Seems to me my reputation is worth a helluva lot more than what you're offering."

"You already agreed to the terms."

"Did I? Or did you throw them out and I didn't argue?"

"Now isn't the time for a renegotiation."

"I'm not negotiating. I know what I want. I want to expose you for what you really are. I want you to get kicked out of the business and Darren barred from competing for having worked with you to fix contests."

"What the hell are you talking about?"

"I'm talking about playing the long game. Preserving the sanctity of the sport. Keeping assholes like you out of it."

"I've been in this sport for longer than you've been alive, kid."

"Seems to me you've been in it long enough."

The recording grows muffled then. There's the sound of a scuffle, Cole's voice shouting, *"What are you doing?"* and then a murky silence.

"Oh my god," Darren whispers.

Gabriel stares at the phone like if he looks hard enough he might be able to see as well as hear what's happening.

I reach for the phone and pause the recording. "You don't want to listen to this." I pull the phone from his grip and hand it to one of the officers.

"I didn't mean to kill the kid," Alan wails suddenly. "I was just trying to scare him."

"Cole was just pretending to go along with it so he could record Alan's offer." Gabriel's hands are shaking. "This phone—that recording—that's what Cole died for."

"Why hang on to the evidence?" I ask. "Why didn't Alan toss it before now?"

"What better place to get rid of it than in the middle of the Atlantic?" Pope gestures to the ferry, and I nod. Alan must've been planning to toss Cole's phone over the edge of the boat somewhere between the OBX and the mainland, never to be found. When it seemed like he might not make it to the ferry after all, he was willing to settle for the end of the dock.

Darren lunges for his manager, landing a punch squarely on his jaw. The officers standing on either side of Alan try to hold Darren off.

"What the hell?" Darren shouts. He turns to Gabriel, his chest heaving. "I had no idea," he says, sounding as though he's almost begging Gabriel to believe him. "I'm not a cheater, and I would never, ever have hurt Cole. Not like that."

The horn from the ferry blasts, indicating that it's about to pull away from the dock. With the officers focused on Darren, Alan must see an opportunity to escape, because he starts to run all over again. This time, he's headed toward a small speedboat parked at the side of the dock.

Gabriel catches the back of Alan's jacket. I hear it tear. Darren dives for Alan's feet. Alan tumbles to the ground.

The officers catch up. I guess it's not surprising that Gabriel and Darren—two professional athletes—are in better shape than the Kildare County Police Department. Finally, one of them slaps a pair of handcuffs on Alan and leads him off the dock. The other reaches for me and undoes the handcuff dangling from my left wrist like a bracelet.

"We'll need you to come in for questioning," he shouts over his shoulder as he walks away. I'm not sure if he's talking to Darren, Gabriel, Pope, or me. Maybe all of us.

Darren sinks to the ground, sitting cross-legged on the dock.

"I can't believe Alan would do that." Darren looks tearful.

"What are you crying for? You'll find another manager," I spit out.

Darren shakes his head solemnly. "I know Cole and I got into it, but . . . I've been surfing with him my whole life. We traveled to the same contests. My mom knows his mom, you know?" He presses his hands into the wood beneath him, wincing when he hits a splinter. "He made me a better surfer."

I remember how distraught Darren sounded the morning after Cole's body was found. I'd thought it was sour grapes over losing the spotlight to Cole's disappearance and concern over how he would come off. But actually, he had just been crushed that his best, long-standing competitor had died. They may have been rivals, but Darren respected Cole.

Darren pushes himself up to stand and holds his hand out for Gabriel to shake. "I'm going to donate my winnings from this contest to charity, in Cole's name."

Gabriel hesitates. There's a shadow of doubt on his face, like he's not entirely convinced that Darren wasn't in on Alan's dastardly plans. But then there's something else, too. The recognition that when Cole died, Darren lost something, too.

Slowly, Gabriel nods and takes Darren's hand.

"I'm so sorry, man," Darren says.

"Me, too," Gabriel agrees. "Me, too."

CHAPTER 35

KIE

I HESITATE BEFORE OPENING THE DOOR. I'VE BARELY SPOKEN to my parents since our fight the morning of the tow-in contest, the day after my epic wipeout—since before Cole went missing and was found dead. And the conversations we did have weren't exactly calm and rational.

That seems like a thousand years ago.

The last thing I want to do is face my parents right now. But the idea of going anywhere but home is somehow even more exhausting. I can't remember the last time I slept through the night. Slowly, I walk up the steps of our white house, perched above the marshes.

It's early enough that at least Mom will still be home, having breakfast in the kitchen. There's no way to tiptoe into the house without being seen.

I take a deep breath and open the glass back door with its million-dollar view. I walk across the living room and into the bright open kitchen. Mom's sitting at the table, coffee cup in hand. I feel my stomach lurch with hunger.

Mom stands. She's in her bathrobe, her dark hair messy around her face.

242

"So, she's alive. If you're going to be out all night doing god knows what with god knows who, the least you could do is call."

She thinks I was out partying all night. Having fun. Getting into trouble with the other Pogues.

"Where's Dad?" I ask.

"At The Wreck. Early delivery. Someone was supposed to be helping out with that kind of thing this summer," she adds pointedly. "We called the school. It took some doing, but they agreed to take you back in the fall."

"What?"

"We discussed this, Kiara. You haven't shown up to work in days. Your actions have consequences."

"I can explain—"

"I don't want excuses, young lady. At least when you're enrolled in a good school, we know you'll be away from—"

"From Pope and John B and JJ?" I finish for her. "Like Kooks are good influences? Let me tell you about the party at Ryan Bradley's the other night—"

"We've been worried sick, and you've been party-hopping!" Mom screeches.

"I thought you'd be pleased that at least the party was on the right side of town," I answer hotly.

Mom takes a step back. She doesn't look like she's gotten any more sleep over the past few days than I have.

"Mom, you don't have to worry about me when I'm with the guys," I explain softly. "The four of us, we take care of each other."

I stop short of telling her it's the Kook guys she should be worried about.

Before Mom can answer, her phone rings. She picks it up, and her eyes widen.

"Yes, sir," she says. "I'll tell her. She'll be there."

"Who was that?" I ask. "The headmaster at KCD? Do I have to do some kind of extra credit assignment to secure my readmission? I'm not doing it."

Mom sits back down at the kitchen table, takes a long sip of her coffee. "Do you mind telling me why the police are looking for you?"

I sink into the seat across from her. "What do you mean?"

The battery on my phone is dead. If they tried calling me directly, I missed it.

"That was the sheriff. Apparently they'd like you to come in to make your statement this afternoon."

"I can explain that."

Mom shakes her head, as if there's not an explanation in the world that could make her feel better.

I reach across the table, pull her hands from her coffee mug and take them in mine. "Mom, please listen to me. The police want to talk to me because a friend of mine was murdered. You know Cole, the surfer who was found dead a few days ago?"

Mom nods. Everyone on the island knows about Cole.

"He was murdered, and my friends and I helped find the person who killed him."

Instead of looking impressed like I expected, Mom looks horrified. "What kind of danger did you put yourself in, Kiara?"

"I was never in danger because I was never alone. My friends were with me every step of the way. And I was with them. Can you understand that? How much my friends mean to me?"

Mom doesn't answer me.

"Mom, please. I know you're frustrated. I know Dad's pissed that I missed work. But I promise, I had a good reason for it. I won't miss another day of work for the rest of the summer. Please, please don't make me go back to that school. I was miserable there."

Mom sighs. "Do you know how much I wanted to go to that school when I was your age?"

I nod. "I know. But I'm not you, Mom. I don't want the same things you wanted. I don't have the same dreams. But I do have dreams. Big dreams. And maybe I should've told you about them. Maybe I should've told you how much I love my friends, and surfing, and this island. I know all about your dreams—where you wanted to go to school and live, and how much you wanted to marry Dad and turn The Wreck into a success. And because I know all that, I understand you. So maybe it's not your fault that you don't under-stand me. 'Cause I never told you about all the things I want."

Mom's eyes go wide, filling with tears. I guess this is the most I've talked to her in a while that isn't screaming and shouting across the house while I race out the door.

"Please, Mom. Please don't make me go back to that school. That's the thing I want most right now—to finish high school with my friends."

Mom pulls her hands from mine and leans back in her chair. I brace myself for her to lay down some kind of ultimatum. But instead she says, "I'll talk to your father," which is better than the *absolutely not* I'd been expecting.

I throw myself across the table and hug her. She's startled, but after a moment she hugs me back. I'd forgotten how good it feels, being hugged by my mom.

CHAPTER 36

KIE

"C'MON." GABRIEL GRINS. "I PROMISED TO TEACH YOU to tow-in."

It's nearly dinnertime, but the sun's still bright overhead. Gabriel, Pope, and I are leaving the police station, having given our official statements. Somewhere inside, Alan's locked in a holding cell.

"You're leaving tomorrow," I remind him. Really, I'm reminding myself. After the last few days, it almost feels like Gabriel is one of the Pogues.

"All the more reason to get out on the water tonight," Gabriel says. He grabs my hand and pulls me away from the station. Pope follows.

※ ※ ※

JOHN B'S BEHIND THE WHEEL ON THE *POGUE*, STEERING US back to the off-shore waves where the tow-in contest took place a few days ago. Gabriel follows in the *Pogue*'s wake on a Jet Ski.

"I still can't believe you guys slept in the morgue without us," JJ moans.

"I can't believe it's the 'without us' part you're focused on," I reply. "You could've just said I can't believe you guys slept in the morgue and left it at that."

"You can't blame JJ for being pissed." John B has to shout to be heard over the roar of the motor and the waves. "We're not used to the two of you going off on an adventure without us."

"Well, I promise not to do it again."

"That's all I ask," JJ says. "It's not like I'm being unreasonable. Pogues are supposed to share their adventures."

I grin, but there's a sadness to my smile. Because I know—and even JJ knows—that there are some adventures the four of us can't share.

Like this one, right now. I zip myself into my wetsuit and throw my surfboard over the side of the *Pogue* and pick up the towrope attached to Gabriel's Jet Ski. JJ and John B and Pope can watch me, but they can't take this adventure alongside me.

"You ready?" Gabriel asks.

"No." I straddle my board, my legs dangling in the water. "The last time I took a wave, I wiped out. And that wave was a lot smaller than these ones."

The spray from the waves soaks my skin and hair. These waves aren't clear and glassy like the waves in the tow-in videos I've watched online—the ones off the coast of Mexico and Hawaii, the water warm and tropical aquamarine. They're not nearly as tall as they were the day of the contest (thank goodness), but still, they're bigger than any wave I've surfed before. The water is dark blue and opaque, cold and choppy. This is the Atlantic, not the Pacific.

Which is all the more reason to do it today. Chances like this don't come to the OBX that often.

"I know," Gabriel says. "And it's scary, getting back on the water after a wipeout."

"A *big* wipeout," I correct.

Gabriel smiles. "But the girl I've gotten to know over the past week isn't the kind of girl who lets fear stop her."

"So I'm just supposed to stop being scared?"

Gabriel shakes his head. "No way. Fear has a purpose. It's telling us something. You gotta listen to your fear. So listen—is your fear telling you that you should get back into the boat, today isn't the day for you to tow-in? Or is it telling you that today is the day? Sometimes what we think is fear is really excitement. But you gotta learn how to tell the difference."

What is Gabriel talking about, listening to my fear? It's hard enough to hear his voice over the roar of the ocean. Still, I think about how scared I was in the morgue last night; my fear wanted to get the hell out of there, but some other part of me wanted to stay—to keep watch over Cole, to comfort Gabriel, to do the right thing.

I close my eyes and put my hands on my stomach. I can feel the fear twisting my belly into knots. This is different from the nerves I felt the day of the contest. That day, I was thinking about winning, earning the prize money, finding a sponsor. Today, there's no one watching but my friends. Technically, there's nothing to gain. But the stakes feel even higher in this moment than they did then. This is my chance, even more than that day.

And I begin to feel something else, something that's quieter but every bit as strong. And I know that nothing's going to keep me from taking this wave today.

I open my eyes.

"Okay," I say. "I'm ready."

Gabriel grins and revs the Jet Ski's engine. I tighten my grip on the tow-rope and pull myself up to stand.

And then we're on the wave. Gabriel pulls me over the top just as it starts to swell, then across the choppy surface. Just before it crests, I drop the rope and then I'm riding—by myself, but not alone, because my friends are with me.

And as long as they're here, I don't have to be afraid.

Maybe it's my imagination—because how could I possibly hear anything over the roar of the water?—but I swear I can hear JJ and John B and Pope cheering for me from the *Pogue*. The wave crests above me, curling over me so that I need to crouch down, one hand against the water like I'm leaning into a wall.

The wave crashes over me, but I keep my feet beneath me, riding straight through to the other side, where Gabriel is waiting to tow me back to my friends.

I climb on the back of the Jet Ski, stowing my board behind us.

"What'd you think?" Gabriel asks, but I can tell he already knows the answer.

I put my arms around his waist and hold on as he turns the ski around.

"I think I want to do it again," I answer, squeezing him tight.

CHAPTER 37

POPE

I'VE NEVER SEEN ANYTHING LIKE THIS. JJ SAYS THAT THE waves were even bigger the day of the contest, and I can't quite imagine it. I mean that literally: I can't picture it. I know there are bigger waves out there, and I know that surfers travel the world in search of the elusive hundred-foot wave, but I cannot picture a surfer on a wave that size. It's *unimaginable* to me.

But not to Kie. Watching her take a second wave, I know that she believes in the hundred-foot wave; she can picture it, and she wants to ride it someday.

Even more unimaginable: I can't believe my dad did this. I can picture him young—that's easy, I've seen photographs. And I can picture him in the ocean—that's easy, too: He taught me to swim when I was a kid. But I can't picture him on a surfboard, even in the shallows, let alone on a Jet Ski in the depths.

Scientific Question: Can someone you thought you knew as well as you know yourself turn out to have a side of him that you not only didn't know but can't conceive?

Hypothesis: If Dad could hide such a big part of himself from me, then does it mean I never really knew him at all?

When the police said that Dr. A confessed, I was devastated. Not just because it turned out my mentor was a liar, but because it turned out she wasn't the person I thought she was: a good person, a responsible doctor. I replayed all our conversations in my head: all the things she'd taught me, all the advice she'd given me. Not just about work, but personal things, too. I thought she was wise and kind.

Scientific Question: What good is getting to know people if they can always hide pieces of themselves from you?

Hypothesis: If people can hide bits and pieces of themselves, then is it possible to ever truly know another person?

When Gabriel brings Kie back to the *Pogue* on the Jet Ski, Kie is smiling wider than I think I've ever seen her smile before.

"What do you say, JJ?" Gabriel asks.

"Hell yeah!" JJ shouts, diving off the *Pogue* and into the water. Within seconds, Gabriel's towing JJ into a wave just like he did for Kie.

Kie cheers as hard and loud for JJ as we did for her.

"Oh my god, I've never felt anything like that," Kie says breathlessly. "I'm so glad that storm blew these waves over here."

I stop myself from explaining how storms and waves actually work.

"And glad Gabriel was here to tow you in," I add.

"Yeah," Kie agrees, her smile still wide. "That, too."

Scientific Question: Is it possible to hate someone you also like?

Hypothesis: Gabriel seems like a truly nice guy. He risked everything
to find out what really happened to his best friend. But nothing I've
ever done has made Kie smile like that. So I like him and hate him
both at the same time.

Conclusion: It's impossible to understand just how many emotions the
human brain can hold all at once.

"Do you wish you were going with him?" I ask.

"Huh?" Kie says, her eyes on JJ. She throws her arms over her head as he
tows in.

"Do you wish you were traveling the world like Gabriel, chasing the planet's best waves?"

"Of course I do," Kie answers like it's obvious. "Don't you?"

"Me? I don't want to be a surfer."

"I didn't mean surfing. I mean college, med school, becoming a medical
examiner and solving murder mysteries. That's your dream, right?"

"Right." I nod, and Kie turns to face me, even though it means missing JJ
finish riding the wave. We don't say anything, but an understanding passes

between us: We both have dreams that will take us away from the OBX someday, away from the Pogues.

There's no telling where we'll end up or how much longer the four of us
will be together like this.

Conclusion to Earlier Scientific Question: I know Kie. I know John B,
and I know JJ. I know them like I know myself. Therefore, it is possible
to truly know another person.

And I know Dad, too. Because even though it's impossible to imagine him
on the water, it's not hard to imagine his loyalty to the best friend he lost. It's
the same devotion he has for Mama and for me.

It's a warm, sunny day, but the breeze off the ocean is chilly, making
me wish I had something more than shorts and a t-shirt on. I feel goose
bumps spring up on my arms and legs. Mama used to say that when you
get goose bumps it means someone is walking across your grave, an
expression that never made sense to me—not for its superstition, but
because how could someone walk across your grave while you're still alive
above the earth?

The sound of the Jet Ski roaring back toward the boat makes Kie finally
look away. She jumps back into the ocean.

"My turn!" she shouts, and Gabriel tows her onto another wave.

John B slaps me on the back. "Can you believe your father used to do this?" He nods toward Gabriel.

"Yeah." I smile. "I can."

✳ ✳ ✳

BY THE TIME I GET HOME, IT'S DARK. POP'S SITTING IN THE kitchen with a beer in hand, the newspaper spread out in front of him.

"Do I want to know where you've been?" he asks.

That's his way of asking if I want to tell him.

I pull out the chair across from Pop. "Tell me about Howie."

Pop looks up, startled to hear his old friend's name. But a slow smile spreads across his face. "Craziest sonuvabitch I ever met. The sort of guy who couldn't resist a dare, no matter how stupid. The things I saw him eat because someone offered him five bucks to eat it: a rancid fish washed up on the beach, hot sauce, mystery meat . . ." Pop shudders, but he's laughing, too. Suddenly, Pop's smile fades. "I don't know. Maybe if he'd been more careful . . . But I thought I was careful enough for the both of us."

"Do you miss it? Surfing, I mean."

"Every day."

"Do you ever wish—I mean, I can't believe you gave all that up."

"Didn't see the point, after Howie was gone."

"But you were a pioneer in the sport! You could've traveled the world like all the surfers who've been crowding the island this week."

"Son, when I say I didn't see the point, I don't mean I was too depressed to get back on the water. I mean I didn't *want* to keep taking risks. I'd done that— I'd ridden wild waves and risked my life for it. That part of my life was over. I didn't feel like I was giving anything up. I was ready for the next part."

He looks at me meaningfully. The next part, he means, was Mama, and the store, and me, too.

"How could you keep such a big part of yourself from me?"

Pop laughs. "Son, you telling me that you don't keep any secrets from me?"

Okay, he's got a point there.

His face turns serious as he continues: "The truth is, Pope, it isn't a big part of me anymore. I never felt as though I was keeping some big part of myself hidden. It's an old part of myself that I outgrew. It just doesn't fit me anymore. Maybe you're too young to understand it, but if you live long enough, you'll have different dreams, new goals. I know you think you know exactly what you want your life to be, but that could change on a dime, you mark my words."

I nod. I only half believe him, but the scientist in me knows that my skepticism only proves his point: I'm too young to understand it.

"I never looked back, Pope," Pop says. "And you know what? I loved surfing, but not nearly as much as I love what came after it. Nothing is more important than family."

"Yeah," I agree. I'm thinking not just of Mama and Pop but also of Kie and John B and JJ. Of Gabriel and the risks he took for his best friend.

I'm crushed that Dr. A—my mentor, the person I thought I wanted to be just like when I grew up—lied on an autopsy report. But she did it to protect her brother. The truth is, I would risk my job for John B, JJ, and Kiara. In the last few days, I *did*.

The difference is they would never do something as heinous as what Alan did and then ask me to help them get away with it. But it would be a lie to insist that I'd never break the rules for my friends—for my family—just like Dr. Anderson did.

I'm going to leave the island one day, like Kie said, for college and med school and whatever comes after that. But the Pogues will always be my family. Which means the island will always be my home.

"I love you, Pop," I say. He looks even more surprised than when I asked about Howie. I don't think either of us remembers the last time I said the words out loud.

"I love you, too, son," Pop says. He puts his hand on my knee and squeezes. "I love you, too."

CHAPTER 38

KIE

"I WISH I COULD TAKE YOU BACK OUT THERE," GABRIEL SAYS wistfully. "But the storm's long passed."

I nod in agreement. It's hard to believe, but if Gabriel and I took a boat to the same spot in the ocean that was peppered with walls of waves just a day ago, the water would be glassy and smooth. We're sitting in the courtyard of his motel in the yellow early-morning light. There's a duffel bag at Gabriel's feet and a long canvas bag the shape of a surfboard propped against the lounge chair opposite us.

"How do you get that thing on a plane?" I ask. Gabriel's taking the ferry back to the mainland, then catching a flight to the competition in Costa Rica. After that, he says, he's going home to Brazil for a few weeks.

"I have to check it," Gabriel answers. "It's the worst, because what if they lose your luggage? Can you imagine getting to a contest and not being able to enter because your board's somewhere else?"

I shake my head. I can't imagine. I've never surfed anywhere but the OBX.

"Just you wait," Gabriel says. "You'll be worried about that kind of stuff just like me before long."

I grin.

The sound of a horn honking brings us to our feet. It's the Twinkie. John B, JJ, Pope, and I are driving Gabriel to the ferry.

We're all quiet on the drive to the docks. I wonder if Gabriel's thinking of the last time we were here.

"Will Darren be in Costa Rica?" Pope asks as John B pulls into a parking spot.

Gabriel shrugs. "I don't know. But either way, I'll see him again soon. Miss one contest, you still make it to the next, or the one after that."

"Is it hard," Pope asks, "traveling all the time?"

"I'm sure it's lonely out there," JJ adds.

"Yeah, I get homesick, but I think that's a good thing."

"How is that a good thing?" I ask.

"Because it reminds me I have a home to go to. Some of these guys, they don't really have a home base. But I'm lucky. No matter what happens, I can always go back home."

I lock eyes with JJ, Pope, and then John B through the rearview mirror. I know we're all thinking the same thing: We're lucky, too. No matter what happens, we'll always have a home here on the island. We'll always have a home with the Pogues.

"I better get a move on," Gabriel says, opening the passenger-side door.

"Good luck out there," John B says, and shakes Gabriel's hand. JJ goes in for a hug.

"Thanks for all your help, JJ," Gabriel says. "You're wild. Stay wild."

Pope passes him his enormous surfboard bag.

"Hey, man, I just want to say thank you again. I know how much you risked to help me. Guess your internship is officially over, huh?"

"Considering that my mentor is in the process of losing her medical license and I'm the reason why, yeah." Pope grins. "It was worth it, though. I'm glad I could help. I mean, not glad," Pope stutters. "Of course I'm not glad any of this happened—"

"I know what you mean." Gabriel grins, clapping Pope on the back. "And thank you."

Gabriel turns to me, and I get the idea he's about to thank me, too—for blowing off work, even though it pissed off my parents, in order to help him.

I speak before he can. "I'll walk you to the ferry," I offer, climbing out of the van without giving him a second to argue.

"Say goodbye to your old man," Gabriel calls to Pope over his shoulder as we walk from the parking lot toward the water.

"I will," Pope promises. Even though Gabriel's back is to Pope, he raises one arm, like a salute to Heyward.

"Did you mean it?" I ask softly as we approach the ferry. I feel the splinters of the dock beneath my bare feet.

"Mean what?"

"Earlier, when you said I'd have to worry about losing my board someday—do you really think I'm good enough? Tell me the truth. I promise it won't hurt my feelings if the answer's no. I'd rather know."

Gabriel stops walking, so I do, too. He puts his board and duffel bag on the wooden planks beneath us and turns to face me, placing one hand on each of my shoulders. We've spent so much time together over the past few days, rushing from one place to the next, that I feel like I haven't really *looked* at him since the day we met. Now, I let myself take him in: his dark brown hair and light brown eyes, the tan lines etched into his face.

"You saw me wipe out," I remind him.

"I told you, even the best surfers wipe out from time to time. Wiping out doesn't mean you're no good. It means you're pushing yourself to be better."

"Yeah, but am I good enough?"

"You don't strike me as the sort of person who needs someone else to tell her she's good enough."

He's right. I'm not. But in the world of competitive sports, your opinion of yourself isn't always enough to make it to the finish line. You have to impress managers, judges, sponsors, if you want to make a living.

"It helps when someone else believes in you, too," I explain.

"You're right about that," Gabriel agrees. "Sometimes I forget how lucky I am. My parents never tried to get me to do anything else."

"My parents are still hoping this is all a phase I'll outgrow."

I don't just mean surfing, but the Pogues, too, and my entire personality.

"Well, Kiara, if you want my opinion, I'll give it to you—though I know you don't *need* it. I think you're good. I meant it when I said that one day you'll be lugging your board through baggage claim on the other side of the globe just like me. You are the type of person who's going to get to anywhere she wants to go."

My lips widen into a smile. "I wish I were going with you." I nod in the direction of the ferry. "I don't mean, like, *with you*, with you. I meant that I want to leave with you to go surfing."

"I wish you were coming with me, too," Gabriel says. "And not just to surf."

I feel my cheeks grow warm as he leans down. I tilt my face up to meet his.

"With everything that happened, I never had a chance to do this," Gabriel whispers. Then he presses his lips against mine.

I hesitate for a split second, but then I lean in, wrapping my arms around his neck. The kiss shifts into a hug so tight it's like this hug isn't just a hug but a promise.

The ferry horn blows, reminding us that Gabriel and I can't stand here forever. Finally, Gabriel pulls away.

"See you around," Gabriel says, and I understand just what that hug was trying to say. Not *goodbye*, but *I'll see you again*.

"See ya," I answer. Gabriel picks his bags up off the ground and walks away without looking back. I watch him step on the ferry, watch the boat float away.

Then I turn on my heel. John B, JJ, and Pope are all standing next to the van, pretending they weren't just watching the whole time.

"You okay?" Pope asks as we all climb into the Twinkie.

I consider the question. I wiped out at the contest, and my parents are pissed as hell for the days of work I missed and the nights I didn't come home. I spent the night with a dead body, and the guy I like just floated away. The big tow-in waves have vanished; it could be years before we get a storm that creates waves like that again. I promised my mom I'd show up for the lunch shift today, even though all I want to do is grab a board and race into the water.

But I'm driving off in a van with my best friends, and we're going to the Chateau, and the sun is shining.

I roll down the window, the breeze blowing my hair in every possible direction. I turn to John B, JJ, and Pope and grin. And for a moment, I think about how if there's one thing I'm thankful for other than getting to meet Gabriel, it's them. The family that I walked into when I needed it the most, who hold me together in all the best ways and through all the waves.

"Yeah," I say, and I mean it. "I'm good."